Kill

Hollows

By S.D. Lifter

the Token-Oak Series

Book One

For Abby, Lily, and Lincoln

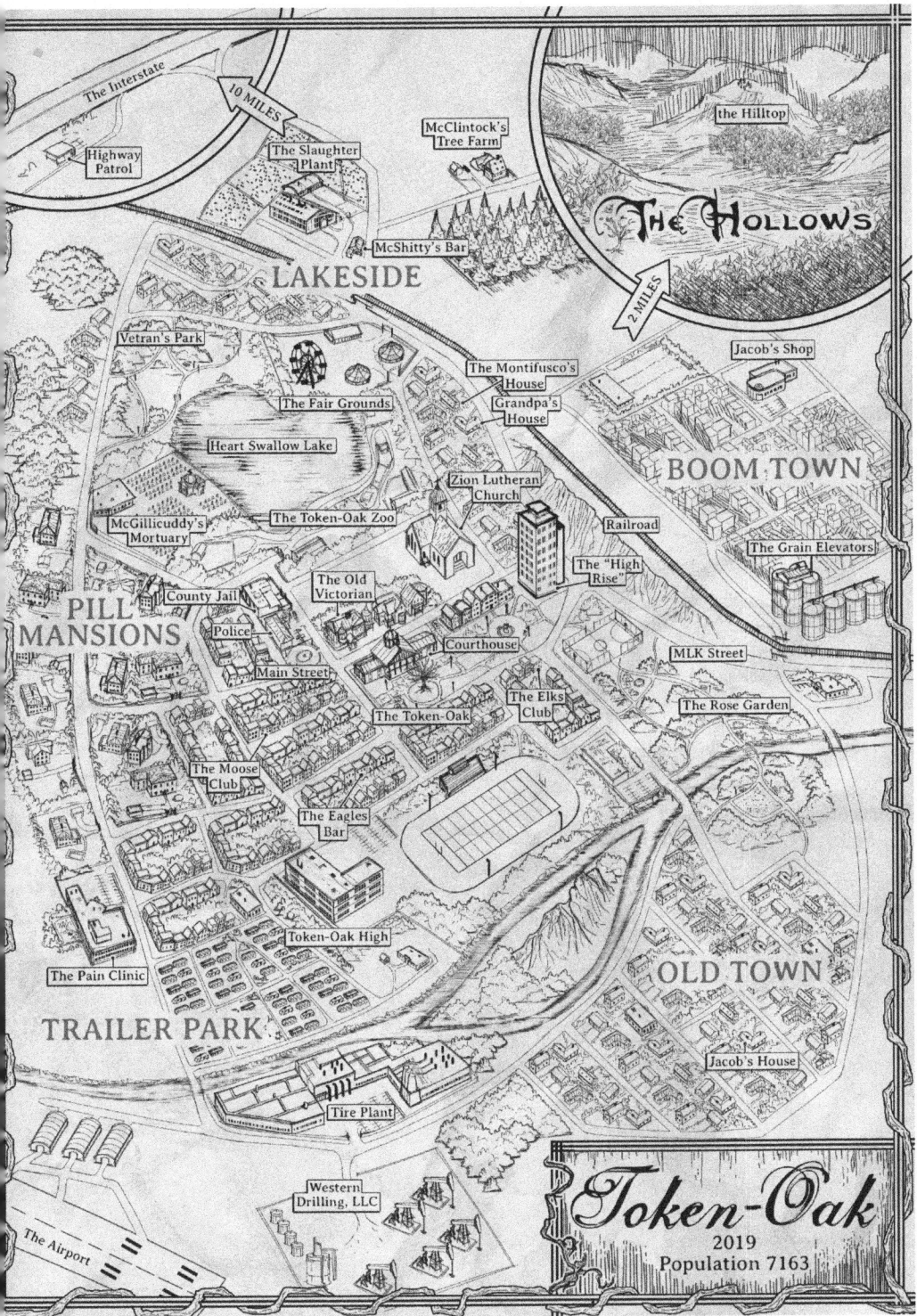

The Interstate

10 MILES

Highway Patrol

The Slaughter Plant

McClintock's Tree Farm

the Hilltop

The Hollows

2 MILES

McShitty's Bar

LAKESIDE

Jacob's Shop

Vetran's Park

The Montifusco's House

Grandpa's House

The Fair Grounds

BOOM TOWN

Heart Swallow Lake

Zion Lutheran Church

McGillicuddy's Mortuary

The Token-Oak Zoo

Railroad

The Grain Elevators

The "High Rise"

The Old Victorian

PILL MANSIONS

County Jail

Police

Courthouse

MLK Street

Main Street

The Rose Garden

The Token-Oak

The Elks Club

The Moose Club

The Eagles Bar

Token-Oak High

The Pain Clinic

TRAILER PARK

OLD TOWN

Jacob's House

Tire Plant

Western Drilling, LLC

The Airport

Token-Oak

2019
Population 7163

CHAPTER 0

THE NIGHT OF THE SYNDEMIC
October 31, 2020

"We've got a bunch of calls coming in about smoke at the Pain Clinic. Johnnie, what's your 20?" snapped the radio between Officers John Brady and Susan McMillian in squad car three. There was a ride-along, a DTF trainee visiting from Kanas City, in the seat behind the officers in the cage. Officer Brady looked over at his partner in the passenger seat and raised his eyebrows.

"It's your favorite place, McMack. That clinic's a dumpster fire."

"Probably a junkie pissed they wouldn't write a script," McMillian bit her lip and shrugged as she examined the smoke roiling in the distance.

"That clinic has never turned down a script," Brady said with a sneer. "Never."

Brady grabbed the handheld CB and clicked it to life, "Just passing Courthouse Square on Shiloh Street. We're on the way. *Over*," Brady said as he hit the lights on the squad car, bathing the dead, twisted limbs of the old oak tree in the center of town in a lurching, nystagmic pattern of red and blue. The siren's hollow echo reverberated off the pillars of the limestone courthouse, and the police cruiser's engine roared as they raced up Shiloh Street.

From the moment he woke up that morning, Brady had an unsettling sensation in his guts; a queasy feeling his grandma used to call the "nervous

1

shits." He had patrolled the streets long enough to know you *listen* to those feelings. Tension hung over Token-Oak like low-hanging funnel clouds in the middle of May. Yesterday's overdoses and the dead trees everywhere gave Brady a chill. Something was in the air. Something was coming.

By the pricking of my thumbs, Brady thought, remembering a line he memorized for a school play years ago. He shook his head and tightened his grip on the wheel.

He saw a pillar of baby blue smoke roiling in the streetlights in the distance.

Chemicals, Brady thought, *damn*. This was no gas fire or stalled car that burst into flames. This was something industrial.

"What the fuck is burning?" asked McMillian, her eyes locked on the sky ahead.

Of course, it was the Clinic, it was always the goddamned Clinic, Brady thought. For a town of seven thousand, Token-Oak had a Pain Clinic that treated thirty-five patients at a time and had a waiting room that could serve 200. Patients came to the clinic from the surrounding eight counties to get their prescriptions. Most days, the line for the clinic stretched around the building and down the sidewalk. It had the foot traffic of a methadone clinic in Chicago or New York not what you'd expect in some little town in the rolling hills of the Great Plains.

For years, Brady thought meth was the worst thing that could happen to a small town. Meth got a person high for days. Dopers made it with household chemicals. But only *dopers* took meth. Opiates, however, were legal and everyone from the local preacher to a handful of county commissioners were hooked on oxy. Some days, to Brady, it seemed like Token-Oak had just three types of folks: those addicted to the shit, those selling it, and the rest who didn't leave their houses at night and slept with loaded pistols on their nightstands.

Officer Brady looked back at the ride-along, Tim Forsyth, a Drug Task Force officer in training, and wondered if he even had to shave every day. The powers that be had sent Forsyth to the prairie to learn about small-town drug networks, and on last night's shift, the kid got a crash course in rural drug interdiction: two meth explosions over in Boom Town, a drug-related homicide in the trailer park, and even a flock of runners with several hundred gallons of anhydrous on MLK out by the fairgrounds. To top the night off, there were a half dozen ODs. Local addicts had mixed meth and oxy and were shooting it up with disastrous consequences: Six dead, and a dozen more lay writhing in hospital beds with their veins on fire. Brady saw fear in Forsyth's eyes that night. The Big City cop who came to little old Token-Oak to learn.

Jesus, Brady thought as he looked at the kid in the rearview biting his lip and wringing his hands, *welcome to Token-Oak, kid.*

"Put your seatbelt on, Timmy," Officer Brady said as he gunned the cruiser towards the blaze. The car sped through intersections and passed the bar crowd at the local Moose club, a collection of local drunks gave fascist salutes as the cruiser sped past.

"Will you look at that?!" Officer McMillian exclaimed as the fire came into view.

Brady keyed the mic on the radio, altering dispatch, "Jack, we've got definite flames at the Clinic. Looks bad."

The Pain Clinic was raging. Ten-foot flames were dancing into the night air through a small hole in the roof. Dozens of people packed the sidewalk watching the blaze. They didn't run, officer Brady thought, because they didn't want to lose their place in line.

As the cruiser rolled into the parking lot of the Pain Clinic, there was an acrid odor so overpowering that Brady had to cover his mouth with his handkerchief. His eyes watered, and his lungs burned. He slammed on the brakes.

"*What is that smell?*" Forsyth said from the back seat.

"Fucking ammonia," McMillian coughed as she hit the button to open the trunk. "I'll get the respirators. We need to clear those dumbasses away from the fire."

As Brady reached down for the CB, a torrent of hot air ripped its way out of a hole in the roof. A blast of flaming debris shot out a hundred feet in every direction. Flames rained down on the shuffling crowd as they stood watching the inferno. The ground shook, and a sinister hiss shrieked through the night air.

"Damn!" McMillian said, "Why the hell are those people not running?" McMillian opened the passenger door and slid out of the cruiser, scrambling towards the open trunk. The backs of the crowd alternated in a strobe of red and blue.

Brady clicked the megaphone to life and shut off the siren to the cruiser. "*YOU PEOPLE, GET THE HELL BACK!*"

A hundred faces snapped towards the police cruiser. They had their heads ducked and legs bent in a crouch. The image that flashed in Brady's mind was of an attack dog: roiled, hackles up, ready to bite. Brady had seen a shit-ton in his time on Token-Oak PD, but he had never seen anything like the way this crowd acted. His hand instinctively reached to the holster of his gun. He checked his belt for an extra magazine.

Forsyth desperately whispered from the back seat, "*McMillian should—she—she should get back in.*"

The crowd lurched, suddenly, in a singular movement. In disbelief, Brady blinked twice and pulled his head back to refocus his eyes. The group—every single person—broke into a violent sprint toward the cruiser. Their eyes were wide open, their fingers outstretched. All of them were screaming, mouths open and tongues churning, the veins on their necks bulged and muscles stretched like taut cables.

Susan put her palm on the edge of the trunk and slammed it shut. She looked at the clinic as she rounded the cruiser. A hundred faces were looking back at her. Not just looking, *glaring*. She slowed, then stopped and tilted her head, the respirators dangling from her hand.

"No," she murmured.

There, incredibly, in the middle of the crowd, she saw her nephew, Parker. He had just turned seventeen, and no one had seen him in over four months. Around his neck, he wore the coral beaded choker that she brought back from her honeymoon in the Dominican Republic. Out of all her nephews and nieces, Parker was her favorite. He was the type of kid so full of life that he radiated genuine warmth. His laugh—that out-of-breath, squeaking gasp—could heal any wound. Parker, she was sure, was destined to move out of Token-Oak and pursue a career in something that suited his gregarious nature and inquisitive personality.

Looking at him now, Susan saw that warmth was gone. Parker's eyes were blank; the fire that had burned inside him had been extinguished. He breathed in heavy, panting gasps, and when their eyes met, he did not recognize her, she was sure of it. The throng of people surged toward her. Parker's face contorted as he screamed along with the pack. Susan McMillian stood gobsmacked as she watched her nephew close upon her.

She never even put her hand on her gun.

"*SUSAN!*" Brady yelled out the open window.

The crowd slammed into her and slung her onto the trunk lid. She hit the black paint with a dull thud. A dozen sets of hands grasped at her body. McMillian's screams were cut short as a man grabbed her by the throat and ripped it open, parts of her tongue and trachea dangled in the night air. Officer McMillian gurgled as blood sprayed from her neck. The crowd engulfed her failing body, gutting her like a freshly caught largemouth bass.

Brady pulled his service Glock and fired through his window. He emptied the magazine into a half-dozen people in the crowd. Bodies fell onto the asphalt parking lot. A middle-aged woman shot in the face spilled over the hood of the cruiser. He hit a young man in the chest three times, but he kept coming. They seemed almost oblivious to the gunshots. They leaned into the bullets, not one of them so much as flinched as they moved, always closer.

Brady hit the release on his magazine and reached for another, too late. Grasping hands pulled him out of the window and into the night. Fingers tore at his eyes and face as he squinted and screamed. His left ear was ripped from his head. A young woman, her face a smear of rage, grabbed his nose and split one of his nostrils in half.

When the Pain Clinic exploded it scattered everyone and everything in the parking lot. A hot blast of fire hit his skin, and he, the crowd, and the car were blown back. The cruiser tumbled over once, then again, landing on its roof on Halstead Street.

He opened his left eye to a squint and saw he was lying not far from the upside-down cruiser. He felt the fire on his back, his ears rang, blood poured from a dozen wounds, and he was pretty sure his arm was broken, but at least no one was trying to rip his face off anymore. Looking around he could see the street was a mess of gore and carnage: broken limbs and bodies, some of them burning, littered the black asphalt. Through the smashed windows of the cruiser, he saw dozens of his attackers starting to regain their feet. Some of them were burning too.

What the fuck is happening?

Movement in the back seat of the cruiser caught Brady's eye. Forsyth was slapping at the flames and jumping around the back-seat area. He danced in the fire and the pain, too scared and too panicked to save himself.

The CB on the dash clicked to life. A questioning voice demanded an update. *Jackson?* There was another call, a fire at the High Rise. Brady

5

couldn't make out more than that, but he was sure he heard gunshots in the background.

Through an avalanche of exquisite pain, his final thoughts were those of a man who gave twenty-two years of his life to protecting and serving his community. There were thousands of kids sleeping in Token-Oak. Most of those were little, just toddlers. As he watched the flaming backs of the crowd sprint down Halstead, he thought about protecting those little kids.

Suddenly, the pain was gone, and in his deepening stupor, he looked down Halstead Street and the mansions that lined the road.

"COME IN, ANYONE!" Deputy Sheriff Jackson Gillatrout screamed into the CB sitting on his desk in the Token-Oak Police Station. Four squad cars patrolled the county at large—and none of them had reported in the last half hour. He had lost contact with McMillian and Brady in squad car three at the Pain Clinic. A team of three officers went into the High Rise searching for a shooter. Two squad cars had driven to the overturned fire engine on MLK to investigate the wreckage. He clicked the CB and called for an answer, an update, anything but dead air. Not one of his officers was responding.

Three explosions, one right after the other, shook the building. The lights in the police station flickered and then died. Jackson grabbed a tactical shotgun from the rack and hurtled the front desk. He threw open the door of the Police station and stepped out onto Main Street. The telephone poles on Main had been cut and were blocking the road. Electric and phone lines were down, the cables crisscrossing the pavement. Everywhere he looked the town blazed: the High Rise, the grain elevators, the bell tower of the courthouse, and the church steeple were all on fire. Even the 400-foot cell phone tower in the field by McClintock's tree farm was nothing but flaming wreckage. *Mother of God*, Jackson thought as he surveyed the wreckage.

The Walkie-talkie on his belt crackled to life. It was Officer Betty Ripsome. She had been checking out an alarm call at the water treatment plant; probably a break-in.

"Jack, there are barrels of chemicals poured into the out-flow pits. The water is poisoned. They poisoned the ---" The message stopped short.

6

Before he could answer, Jackson's eyes were drawn to a house just past Main where a group of people crouched outside a burning home. The front door opened and a man in boxers and one sock leaped down the steps to escape the flames. The people in the yard were on him instantly: one of them grabbed "one-sock" in a chokehold, and another used a huge chef's knife to cut him open from his boxers to his sternum. The group disemboweled the guy, manually, yanking his ropey viscera onto the street and yard. Jackson stood in frozen horror as the man slumped to the sidewalk, leg twitching, outside his burning home.

Jackson tightened the grip on the shotgun, and he thought about taking a shot, but as he watched, they moved to the next house on the street. They lit porch of the home on fire and threw makeshift Molotov cocktails in through the windows. Further up the road, he could see another house beginning to burn. The sounds of panicked screaming and chaos filled the night.

Well, great, Jackson thought, *I'm fucked.* He quickly assessed his situation: flames everywhere, no power, no phones, roads blocked, and packs of roving psychopathic arsonists murdering goddamned everything. *I'm fucking dead.*

Jackson slipped back inside the police station and locked the door. He threw the deadbolt and slid a few desks across the floor to block the entrance.

"*Jack?*" It was Betty on the CB again, she sounded desperate.

Just then, a flaming bottle broke the front window of the Police Station and birthed a river of fire on the wall beside him.

He grabbed the CB, "Betty, don't come back here. The town is burning. There are fires everywhere."

The CB in his hand hissed loudly, a mess of static, gunshots, and a hundred whispering voices—a white noise followed by a strange silence, like a guitar amp turned all the way up. It was a magnetic void of sound. In the middle of that void, a deep and resonate voice cut through.

"*Kill them.*"

Jackson blinked as he looked at the CB, *That's not Betty.*

Not-Betty continued louder, "*Cut the power, poison the water, light the gas, and burn the wood. Peel the skin from their faces when they run from their holes. The lucky ones will die clutching their chest.*"

Prologue

Robert Warrington's Journal
Token-Oak, Winter of 2026
2556 days after the Syndemic

People have always obsessed over of the end of things. In America, especially after the dawning of the 21st century, each summer would find Hollywood churning out blockbusters about robot uprisings or AI's becoming vengeful gods. For a decade the most popular show on TV had zombies wandering across the country like herds of buffalo. Walk into any Barnes and Noble, and you could find handfuls of dystopian post-apocalyptic worlds. To be fair, people had plenty of actually terrifying things to worry about: global warming, rising seas, super flu, super volcanoes, giant meteorites, toxins in our food, air, and water. Hell, the sun itself was just a massive flare away from frying all the electronics on the planet and sending us back to the Neolithic Age.

So, we made up our stories, and sometimes we believed them. Y2K scared us enough to change nearly every major computerized system on the planet in an effort we haven't seen since. Somehow, in 2012 someone got it in their head that the end of the Mayan calendar was the literal end, and a ridiculously large group of people thought that that sounded just right.

In 2016 America elected a flop-haired, ersatz billionaire who once casually asked his top ranking general why we didn't 'just use our nukes.' It wasn't uncommon to see "Giant Meteor 2016" bumper stickers. "Prepping" had become so mainstream that there was a store in most shopping malls with freeze dried food and water purification systems. The apocalypse was right around the corner, or so we hoped. And we were right.

The first beast of the apocalypse—methamphetamine—came from Japan in 1893 when a chemist isolated the ephedrine from a plant that eastern cultures had been used since time immemorial. The Nazis gave Pervitin, a synthesized version of ephedrine, to soldiers during World War II and the drug-crazed Wehrmacht blanketed half of Europe in a furious Blitzkrieg. (The soldiers called it "Panzerschokolade"—tank chocolate). The allies soon found out about the wonder pills and began their own research into the use of the drug allowing the tentacles of the beast to spread across to America in the 1950s. It started as a simple pick-me-up, a good time booster that beatnik poets used for fuel. In the 1960s, Americans reveled in meth's depression and weight loss potential. Meth was outlawed in the 1970s by the American government, pushing it underground: relegating its manufacture and distribution to organized crime and hardened drug users. By the late 1980s, clandestine cooks were exploding from the Alaskan Tundra to Lake Okeechobee, Florida. Meth shattered rural American communities like Little Boy's blast flattened Hiroshima. Crystal Methamphetamine is one of the most abused illegal narcotics in the history of the world. By 2010, over a million Americans were using the drug daily.

In 1991, while America was deep in the throes of a half-century-old meth epidemic, another drug started to wreak its havoc. The second beast, "opioids," had legitimate roots: doctor's prescribing it to their patients. Over the years, it had a handful of names: oxy, roxy, fentanyl, black tar, China, chiva, smack, heroin. All were from the same family of opioids.

Unlike meth, opioids reached into all levels of society. It hit housewives just as hard as street users. Unsuspecting patients were prescribed the drug by their trusted family doctor for an injury only to begin the spiral of addiction. People bought it in the mail, off the shadow internet, and had it FedEx'd to their houses. Opioids were everywhere, more ubiquitous than the Golden Arches of McDonald's.

A syndemic, or synergistic epidemic, is the interaction of two epidemics and the exacerbation of their effects. When the meth and opioid epidemics collided, they fed off each other and exponentially magnified the negative consequences. That is the *syndemic* effect. And that is precisely what happened to the Great U.S. of A.

By the spring of 2020 over a quarter million had died as a result of a concoction known as a "goofball," a mixture of meth and opioids heated in a spoon. The high was said to combine the frantic euphoria of methamphetamines with the warm-bath sedation of heroin—a sirens call that was too often fatal: overdoses skyrocketed. Not only was it dangerously seductive, but for some, it seemed to do more—it elicited a rage, a calculating, open-eyed fury coupled with reckless abandonment. Some would wake with the intent to murder, shadows of their former selves with depraved hearts.

There was public outcry and a flurry of class action lawsuits aimed at the pharmaceutical conglomerates and the doctors who wrote the prescriptions. We tried to face the issue by ignoring the reality we had created and distracted ourselves by watching talking heads on twenty-four-hour news networks.

Meth had changed. From the middle of Kansas sprang a new synthesis of meth that, when mixed with an opioid and heated, grabbed peoples' brains and never let them go. It dipped its tentacles deep into the gray matter and molded the perfect soldiers of the apocalypse. Before long, this new meth was everywhere, and the number of afflicted grew unchecked.

The signs were everywhere. While people were helplessly plugged into their phones and sprouting roots into their couches binge-watching Netflix, America was rotting. The epidemic hit the rural Midwest first. The afflicted started to show signs of "the shakes," a twitchy, spastic shuffle that was eerily coordinated across groups of people.

It is a fact that they were dead, but this being the late twenty-teens, facts had little to do with truth. They seemed to exist somewhere between the planes of life and death in some biological limbo. As the number of afflicted began to grow, they formed packs which would murder and burn. The screams and the flames spread across the country like a virus, and the army of the apocalypse grew. I wish I could say that was the worst of it, and perhaps I'll get to all that.

All this shit started in the little town of Token-Oak, my hometown. As a kid in Token-Oak, the meth crisis had just taken hold. When I moved away as an adolescent, I saw it increase a little more each time I returned to the town. Small pockets of the apocalypse—lab explosions, murders, and disappearances—were all over Token-Oak. As an adult that got trapped in that pit of hell, I was at ground zero when the syndemic started. I was in the eye of the hurricane, a silent circle as the ferocious winds of the storm tore the country apart.

I was a child in Token-Oak during the syndemic's humble beginnings in the late 1980s. In a blind stroke of luck, I was a graduate assistant at the University of Harvard when the government first tested human brains for "the shakes." And, somehow, I ended up back home on the day the syndemic officially began. I was at ground zero every step of the way. There is not another person alive or dead that can say the same thing.

If I told you that I don't know why I am writing this book, I'd be lying. It will probably never be read by another human being. There won't be awards, no reading circles, it will not be published. I can tell you that writing these pages at night, nearly drowning in sounds of screaming and the gnashing of teeth, has not been easy. I write this nightly for selfish reasons; It keeps me alive, pushes me to fight on, to scrounge food, and keep my weapons clean.

I am going to take you back to the beginning. All the way back to where it started and walk you through everything; step by bloody step. I'll start with the smartest woman—the most simultaneously ruthless and loving woman that ever lived. And even though we never talked about it, she knew. My grandma knew it was coming and did her best to warn me.

CHAPTER ONE:

BHA-AAB

Robert Warrington's Journal
Token-Oak, Winter of 1991
10,562 days before the Syndemic

When I say my grandma knew the apocalypse was coming, I don't mean it in a general sense. She didn't just foreshadow dark times on the horizon. I believe she saw what was happening: the burning cities, the collapse of agriculture, and corpses along the interstate piled like trash at a landfill. She felt it, too: The intense pressure of knowing ate at her heart and eventually killed her. The incredible weight of this bleak future smothered her before she could adequately warn anyone but me.

She died on a Tuesday right after the wheat harvest. Even in death, the family would say, she accommodated my grandfather's schedule. Grandma planned her own passing—thou the doctors said the aneurysm was a fluke—right down to what she wore to the hospital. One day, Gramps came home from the farm and found her on the sunflower linoleum in the kitchen convulsing. Yet she packed a bag, stashed a week's worth of leftovers in the fridge, and paid the bills a month in advance. Grandma was spooky like that. She had the foresight of a Cajun mystic.

Grandma had these great big eyes, but she rarely opened them more than a squint. She hid them behind reading frames she bought in the plastic turnstile at the local IGA Supermarket. With her head tilted and her reading glasses perched on the tip of her nose, she dug into people with those eyes. She had this way of looking into a person, right inside their thoughts, like she was vetting them for trustworthiness suitable enough to be her confidant. Few met her standards.

Grandma was a collector, like many women from small towns, she had a "power animal." She bought cookie jars, bric-a-brac, and mawkish paintings of her "power animal" that personified her best. For my grandma, it was owls: spooky ass, head-turning-180-degree-Exorcist-style, big-eyed, predatory, nocturnal, clawed, and sharp-beaked owls. The damned things filled her home, lurking in every nook, following you with their eyes. I saw my grandma in all those owls.

Grandma loved to scare little kids. Scare them in a way that was simultaneously welcoming and bone-chilling. Over a plate of fresh-baked cookies—chocolate chip that were puffy, crunchy on the outside, yet doughy in the middle—she'd offer you her "insights" of the world. The cookies lowered your guard and the way she spoke really sucked you in, always in a gentle coo. *"You know, Bob, those black spots on BBQ chips? Those are boogers from people that work at the factory."* Or, ever so subtly, *"I once filled a glass dish with Coke and submerged a metal spoon in it and left it overnight. In the morning, the spoon was gone ... completely dissolved. Now, Bob, imagine what that stuff does to your stomach overnight? Have you been checking your poop for blood?*" And, let's not forget her stories about chocolate, "*that stuff is made from the coco plant, you know, that's where the 'cho' comes from. Well, the plant is used to manufacture illegal narcotics. A little white powder called CHOcaine. There is something in the plant that pulls people in. Changes their brain. Every bit of 'Cho' you ingest is a step closer to being a drug addict when you're older. A step closer to sleeping in gutters, having no teeth, and never wiping your ass with toilet paper. So, enjoy that Butterfinger, Bob, enjoy it real... slow.*"

Yeah, I loved my grandma. Even though she was mean and wrong about a lot of things. I remember her stories because she conveyed them with a quiet passion. She was the only woman I ever met that could scare me to death and make me feel loved unconditionally at the same time.

Grandma grew up in the town of Token-Oak and stayed there her whole life. A town named for the prevalence of thousand-year-old oaks. In its heyday, Token-Oak was a Midwestern postcard town, picturesque in a Norman Rockwell kind of way. In the fall, the foliage from the deep-rooted oaks provided a pallet of Autumn colors so brilliant and varied that people would pull over on the interstate to take family photos with the hills in the background. In recent years, however, the oaks suffered a debilitating disease causing their leaves to fall. These hulking relics stand all over the town leafless and dying, their twisting fingers reaching out into space.

Before things went to hell, townsfolk talked about Token-Oak like a distant relative that once had a multimillion-dollar empire. They never mentioned that the relative spent the fortune on whores and coke only to wind up penniless and using the daily paper as a blanket. Token-Oakeans bragged on the oil booms and the new interstate and the influx of traffic as "progress." They never mentioned the meth labs, violence, and the strange detachment that permeated the town. No one ever discussed the dark underbelly of Token-Oak, no one except my grandma.

Grandma and this will sound crazy, could predict future events. Perhaps not the exact time or outcome, but she could see the future. Frankly, all grandmothers possess this gift in varying degrees of intensity. Most grandmothers can look at a young man and tell you with surprising accuracy if a kid will be a success in life. In a moderately advanced form, some grandmothers can predict the downfall of a kid, but the advanced ones, women like my grandmother, could predict success, downfall, *and* the immediate steps necessary to correct the downward spiral. Grandma had the trifecta, the holy trinity, of grandmotherly prognostication.

Grandma knew where I was headed a long time before I got there. She warned me, and my life happened precisely like she said it would. You see, I was what many considered a smart kid, but one that was intensely troubled by emotions. Back in the Eighties, parents didn't throw around psychobabble. Today, I probably would have landed somewhere on the spectrum. In 1986, I was just a fucked-up little kid struggling through life.

Life was one hell of a struggle.

My dad overdosed when I was six. My mom, my brother—his name was Jacob—and I walked into our trailer on a Friday night after going to the County Fair. Dad was laying on the dirty carpet next to the couch. He had this white froth around his mouth, and one of his eyes was rolled back in his head. In his left hand, he held a hypodermic needle. Mom dropped me in the doorway and released a milk-curdling scream. Jacob and I just stood there, in the living room, looking at Dad.

The whole trailer park was around our house for hours. The cops took Dad away in a black sack and combed through the house looking for more drugs. They took buckets and bottles and dirty tubing out of our back room. Pretty much anything that could be used to make meth.

There was one thing that the cops missed. A few days later, I found a spoon under the couch. The backside was burnt black. The neck of the spoon was wrapped with electrical tape. The bowl of the spoon had a white film, and a piece of cotton singed to it, but it still shined. I'd lay on my twin mattress at the far end of the trailer and look at my upside-down reflection in the concave of that spoon for hours.

My mom caught me with it weeks later. "Where did you get this?" she said in a voice that was somehow a desperate plea and a rage-filled question. I told her that I found it under the couch, "underneath my dad." And Mom cried so long I thought she might have died. But she left me with that dirty spoon.

The next day, Mom went to buy milk at the gas station. A semi-truck hit her car over the bridge by the tire plant. The driver that hit her was so high on meth that he never let off the gas. The roaring engine of the Freightliner slammed her Datsun hatchback over the guardrail and into the icy water of the Smoky River fifty feet below.

In a three-week span, I lost both my parents to drugs. That period changed my life, as you might imagine. Jacob and I went to live with our grandparents. It only took the better part of a week to figure out it was an arrangement that was doomed to fail. Grandma was always watching me, always warning that I couldn't let my past ruin my life. "You drew a rough hand," she'd say, "but you have to persevere. Use this pain, don't let it use you." She was always telling me to "put my suffering to work," like it was a fucking mule that could till a field. She watched me with those huge eyes, like a predatory bird.

I still remember every detail of the afternoon Grandma warned me about the future. And that was decades ago. I was at her house on a chilly October afternoon around my birthday. I was shooting hoops with Jacob just before dinner. We had just finished watching the movie *Hoosiers.* Oh man, we loved to watch movies back then. The final scene was so inspiring to Jacob and me that we ran outside to impersonate the movie protagonist, Jimmy Chitwood. *Hoosiers* meant a lot to Caucasian farm kids in the Midwest. A good jump shot combined with "fundamentals and defense"—and a shitload of freckles—was all it took for your name to be whispered among the wheat stubble for all-time. It was all polished wood and step back jumpers against rowdy-ass opponents. They balled hard in *Hoosiers,* like the NBA in the early '90s, it was football in shorts.

I was ten years old back then. Jacob was twelve.

Jacob and I were adopted by our grandparents late in life. Both were well into their fifties, long past the age when they had the energy to deal with his shit. Jacob's life was a cycle in three repeating patterns: (1) he received little attention, so he did something vicious; (2) he received a beating for his actions that made him worse, and the grandparents felt guilty; and (3) then they showered him with toys and freedom. Jacob was raised by television, and he returned to this well of knowledge again and again. He saw the world through a prism of movie montages and climactic scenes. In this cycle, Jacob developed an innate fixation for creating fear and causing pain. Even at twelve, he was growing into a "special" kid.

We were playing a game of one-on-one on Grandma's driveway. The rotted plywood hoop was just above the garage door. I was smoking Jacob pretty good. He was older, taller, and had the lanky frame of a b-baller but lacked athletic ability. I stole the ball from him regularly, and that really pissed him off.

"Bha-*aaaaaaaab*," Jacob would say in this voice that drew out the vowels like a bone saw. It was a portmanteau word of my nickname and the sound that Jacob said I made when he hit me. There was something about that way Jacob said it, in this sotto voce hiss that was so full of sarcasm and hate: "Bha-*aaaaaaab, don't be a bitch.*" Every time I showed weakness: "Bha-*aaab.*" If I displayed any awkwardness in a social setting: "Bha-*aaab.*" If I was too affectionate with my family pet: "Bha-*aaaab.*" If I flinched when he was about to hit me: "Bha-*aaab.*" That name, said in that voice, came to epitomize everything I hated about myself. It was as if all my adolescent self-reproach came to life when Jacob hissed that name.

Jacob had this weird thing about movies. He'd see it, and he'd do it. Sometimes, when a pivotal scene came on, I'd look over at him, and his face alone was worth the price of admission. His eyes wide, one eyebrow raised in curiosity, and mouth agape in utter fascination. He studied movie characters: their mannerisms, vocabulary, intonation, and style of dress. He lost himself inside that tubed box like no one I'd ever seen before or since. Then he'd head out into the world and imitate. Art became life. Fantasy became a reality. For Jacob, there was never a wall separating make-believe. It was like he existed in this alternate universe that mixed make-believe and real life like fuel and air into a jet engine. He soared into the deep recesses of the back of his mind.

The game, just like in the movie, degenerated into jail ball. It was all hip checks, and awkward curse words dropped by kids who didn't fully understand their meaning. "Nice shot, you damn gigolo" and "you play like you got a tampon in your ass."

Grandma was doing dishes in the kitchen and watching us through translucent curtains. The kitchen window was just up the stairs and overlooked the driveway basketball court. She often sat up there like a silent observer in a booth. I saw her silhouette every time I looked up. One time, I took the ball along the edge of the driveway towards the hoop and Jacob body-checked me into the garage door. The collision made a tremendous noise. Springs, plywood, and metal wheels erupted like a raucous crowd. I hit the pavement cursing up a storm. "What the balls was that, you fucking boot-licking gypsy?!"

I heard Grandma's swollen knuckles and skinny fingers wrapping on the window pane. *Thomp, Thomp, THOMP!* The curtains flew open, and we both saw her scowling down. She had wild eyes that trembled, though the rest of her stood motionless. I could see the air molecules around her head vibrating with energy. Her lips were pursed so tight they could cut through the metal of a spoon. It was a look developed through decades of parenting rowdy kids. It was her own version of the machine kill switch. Flip it, and everything comes to a complete stop.

At least for a while. The thin curtains slowly closed, and Jacob and I started playing again. A shot here. A few dribbles there. I grabbed the ball from Jacob and held it behind me while leaning forward. Both of Jacob's palms faced toward me, his eyes on fire with rage. He looked like a mime performing the trapped-in-a-box routine.

Then we heard some sounds from the end of the driveway. It was the unmistakable clanging of empty gas bottles and the rattle of wrenches against the bed of Grandpa's pickup truck. There was a nasal whine, a seething breath. Whatever it was, it sounded rushed.

I sat the ball down on the pavement and Jacob, and I tiptoed towards the truck.

A man was standing at the tailgate. His head down and his arms furiously rifled through the truck bed. He wore a beanie pulled down to the tips of his eyes. Open scabs dripped blood from his unshaven neck. The skin on his face sagged in loose pouches. His mouth was open, and his lips curled back on his teeth. His black, infected gums puffed outward. There was a filth to him, a layer of grime that indicated he hadn't washed in a long while, maybe months. He wore the clothes of a younger person, but he looked like a haggard old man.

The man grabbed a canister of gas, removed the lid, and dumped out the contents. Gasoline vapors filled the air. Gramps had a 100-gallon tank bolted to the bed of his truck that he filled with anhydrous ammonia, a fertilizer that he used during the growing season. The man grabbed the spigot of anhydrous and twisted it open. The repugnant stench of anhydrous overpowered the gasoline. Jacob and I were fifteen feet away, but even from that distance, the fumes burned my eyes and ignited a burn in my throat. The man coughed and growled through the caustic stench as saliva drizzled from his black gums.

The man wore fingerless gloves. He spilled some of the anhydrous on his skin and yanked a hand away, shaking. The caustic liquid ate away at his exposed flesh, but he did not let go of the hose and stood there until the gascan was full of anhydrous. His eyes squinted hard as he held the can under the spigot. I could smell his flesh burning.

Whenever Grandpa handled the anhydrous, he wore thick rubber gloves and a respirator. Jacob and I must have had eyes as wide as saucers.

When he was finished with the can, he looked up and saw Jacob and me. A loud inhale turned into an animalistic hiss. He was clenching his teeth so hard that his jaw shook. There was a twitch inside him that crawled up from his waist and snarled up his back. His arms and head bobbed and contorted in inexplicable patterns. His eyes swam in their sockets as he tried to focus on us. He had the body of a man, but there was something very inhuman about him. He took heavy and irregular breaths, punctuated by desperate gasps of air. It was like he was fighting inside himself just to live.

He turned away from us as if he heard a sound in the distance. He broke into a run. His limbs stammering and shaking in a disjointed, yet frantic, gallop. He hit the end of the street—two hundred feet—in less than five seconds. The canister of ammonia sloshed caustic liquid in his wake. As he turned into the alley at the end of the street, another figure met him and then a third. They grouped together and disappeared over a dog-eared fence. We watched them run across the railroad tracks and sprint into the grass field by McClintock's Tree Farm.

"What was he doing?" I said, looking up at Jacob. And Jacob had the TV face. His mouth was open, and his head was tilted to one side. His unblinking eyes watched the men disappear over the fence. "Jacob," I said as I reached out to touch him.

Jacob's trance disappeared, and he blinked slow. He turned his head and looked down at me. "He needed that stuff to take back to the Hollows... the anhydrous," Jacob said.

"What was wrong with him?"

Jacob shrugged and looked back at the fence where the man disappeared. "I don't know. Did you hear that fucker breathe? Sounded like a dying cow," Jacob said. And he swiped the ball from me and turned towards the basket.

When we turned, Grandma was standing there holding a double-barreled Winchester. The gun was cracked open, and two fresh shells were resting inside the break action. The brass circles of the shells sparkled in the October sunshine. She stood for a long while intensely watching the men disappear into the tall-grass field.

She grabbed me by the neck and pulled me toward the driveway. I fell, and she kept pulling.

Once we were near the basketball hoop at the far end of the driveway, she let go: "If you were standing at the end of that tailgate, he would have killed you both. If you ever—*ever!*—see a person like that, you run. You get inside the house and lock the doors. There are things in this town, bad things. And don't you think for a minute that just because you're a kid, that thing wouldn't open you up from belly button to Adam's apple."

Grandma took a long breath. She brought her hand to cover her eyes and let out a wobbly exhale. Grandma took me up and hugged me so hard I thought she broke my ribs.

"Why was he breathing like that?" Jacob asked.

Grandma looked back down the drive for a long while. She covered the sun from her eyes as she scanned the fences in the neighborhood. Then she looked at Jacob and I and shook her head. "He breathes like that because he's dying. Been slowly dying for a long time. And one of these days, this whole damn town will be full of people like that."

Grandma pulled the shells from the Winchester and snapped it shut. She slipped the shells in her coat pocket. She looked around and disappeared inside.

Grandma was a woman of idiosyncrasies. She had rules—live or die rules—that she never broke. She wouldn't leave the house at night for any reason. She loved her two Alaskan Huskies, and listened to them like they were people. Responding to each one of their barks while in the house by looking out the shutters to inspect the neighborhood. There was a suspicious side to her, especially people in authority or control. I once saw her bolt from the Token-Oak hospital when a doctor tried to take her blood pressure. "I don't trust him, and neither should you," was all she ever said. It was like she expected the worst in people and searched for it everywhere. For a gregarious kid like me, that coldness was often grating. I could tell that beneath all Grandma's issues, she loved us furiously.

Grandma and I butted heads like two rams on a mountain. She tried to keep me contained, and I was always busting out. She would correct me, and I'd fly off course. It was the ebb and flow of our dynamic.

After Grandma was inside, Jacob looked over at me. "Did you hear that shit? She is losing it," Jacob said in a wobbly, effeminate voice, *"the town will be full of people like that,"* as he imitated Grandma standing with the Winchester. "She needs to be in a place for crazy people."

After a while, Jacob and I were back to jail ball. Within minutes, I caught an elbow to the face and hit the pavement. I sprung up spraying profanities like a yard spreader. The curtains flew open, Grandma was standing in a dark kitchen. A vision of utter rage, she glared down upon us like the demon in Fantasia's *Night on Bald Mountain*.

I was scared, but my anger outweighed my fear. What Jacob did was wrong, he was always wrong. I knew that she saw him, and yet she just stared. Grandma always cut him slack.

I waited until the curtain closed. Then it happened, the middle finger on my right hand extended and my arm shot up until my elbow straightened. Boom. There it was. I flipped my grandma off for only a split second. Turns out, that split second was enough.

Even Jacob, the twelve-year-old sadist, knew I'd made a tremendous mistake.

"You're a dumbass," Jacob said, "she saw that."

"Whatever," I said, holding the ball with both hands while leaning over.

I dismissed the thought and continued the game. Jacob began a new tactic, utterly uncharacteristic. He played softly, no longer pushing me around. It was like he wanted the game to end, just to see what would happen next. After five minutes of disinterested ball, we were done.

Jacob and I kicked our shoes off at the back door of Grandma's house and stomped up the kitchen stairs. Grandma was standing at the sink and washing a set of dishes. Her back was facing me, and she did not offer her usual greeting.

I palmed the handle on the fridge door, yanking it open. A half-full container of cherry Kool-Aid was sitting on the top shelf whispering my name. I stood in the middle of the kitchen pouring the chilled, cherry goodness into a jelly jar. Grandma's back was toward me, her hunched shoulders wiggling as she scrubbed a pot in the sink. Jacob stood at the stove in between us. He had a subtle smile as he watched me.

As I took a drink of the cherry liquid, Jacob was the first to speak.

Jacob said, "Bob bent the garage door."

This was such typical Jacob. His goal in life was to get people to lose it. He was gifted at this skill, like an aikido master throwing an attacking opponent off balance, Jacob knew just where, and how, to press. He kept memories of unhinged emotional responses in his mind like a running back keeps the game ball from a three-hundred-yard game.

"That's bullsh . . ." I said reflexively, only to be interrupted mid-profanity by Grandma's hand. She wheeled from the sink, flattened her palm, and threw a cat-quick right cross. It left the side of my face smashing my cheeks into my molars. All of this occurred in three-tenths of a second. Sometimes, life happens in a flash, but you remember it in excruciatingly slow detail. The way her fingers smashed the fatness of my cheek. How my lips curled as she followed through. The spinning jelly jar full of cherry Kool-Aid. Most of all, though, I remember the crime scene afterward.

Red Kool-Aid splattered all around the kitchen, in patterns so intricate that Jackson Pollock would've been jealous. The sunflower linoleum floor, the finger paintings hanging by magnets on the fridge, even the bubble screen on Grandma's 9" kitchen TV were covered in the pitter-patter Kool-Aid splatter. The red stuff was everywhere, a fine mist of blood like someone's head had exploded. I laid on the linoleum floor looking up at Grandma.

"It was Jacob... he did it," I whimpered from the floor as I pointed at Jacob.

She towered over me with her right hand still cocked. Bending down, she calmed herself, and said the unforgettable words, "You can't control yourself. It's always someone else's fault. And by the time you figure it out, I'll be dead."

Then Grandma leaned down and grabbed me by the collar of my T-shirt, pulled me closer, and said in a hissing whisper, "there is going to come a time, after I am dead when you'll need Jacob. And he'll be there. Family runs deep, and those bonds are forever. All this you're going through is just training *for what's coming*. And when it gets here, you'll be thankful."

Grandma wiped her hands off on a towel and walked out of the kitchen.

Jacob stood by the stove with an orgiastic smile. He had this look, an I'm-in-control-of-a-delicious-situation visage. His smile was so crooked and fulfilled, half his face looked like the Joker from Batman. It was a look that said, "told you so" and "eat shit" with seamless ferocity. The way his upper row of teeth glowed under his upper lip, the evil twinkle in his eye, even the way he held his head slightly upturned and to the side. For a twelve-year-old kid, he could play the douchebag card with uncanny skill.

"Fuck you, Jacob," I said, sulking out of the kitchen.

I heard him laughing hysterically as I descended the basement stairs. He yelled after me, "Ahhh, *Ba-aaaab*, you going to need me someday. You're welcome."

The basement was the furthest spot in the house away from my grandmother, and she needed time to calm. The basement was quiet, had shag carpet, and puffy furniture. The house was not air-conditioned, but the basement was naturally cool. It was a place of respite from family dysfunction and summer heat.

At the base of the stairs, just to the left, there was my grandfather's office. A room unlike any other. Grandpa's U-shaped desk had a glass top. He slid decades of old pictures and newspaper clippings under the glass. It was a tableau of his life and our family history. I sat in Grandpa's office chair with my elbows on the desk, cradling my head in my hands.

Grandpa was a high school history teacher, county politician, and farmer. An avid democrat—the "party of the little people," he always said— he believed in the common man and would rail against the machine any chance that he got. He supported inmates and single moms and small businesses. Most of all, he loved a good underdog story. After all, who is a bigger underdog than farming teacher with four kids and a penchant for taking on societal problems? He even ran for state senate a few times and lost. Badly. Through all his endeavors, he became part of the political machine. He wrote scathing letters to the editor in the local newspaper whenever he saw a person slighted by "big business, big government, or big bullshit." People hated him or loved him. In his office, he kept mementos that he treasured dearly.

The history in that room was personal and honest. On the doorframe, all Grandpa's children had penciled their height from toddler age to present day. Under the glass on the desk, there were hundreds of pieces of paper. One was an article about my great-grandpa who died when his arm was ripped off in a threshing machine. He bled to death in the wheat stubble of our home place field. His last note, scratched with a pocket knife onto a painted piece of John Deere green metal, read: "I love you all. I did my best." There was a photo of my grandfather and Bill Clinton, where Clinton wrote so charmingly, "If I had supporters like you in every state, I'd be king." There were the election results for state senate, where Gramps only brought in 27 percent of the vote, glued to the top of his campaign slogan that read simply: "I teach." Grandpa was so proud of that slogan.

That room was Grandpa's entire life, his sanctuary from the world. A physical manifestation of memories that told his story. There was not a single picture of my grandmother in that office. Other than the scribbled height of the kids on the doorframe, there were no pictures of any of Grandpa's kids either. *His* story.

I sat in that office absorbing the history. My thoughts wandered to what Grandma had said about Jacob. I couldn't envision a scenario when I would need him, the idea that I would be thankful for him was asinine. Just the thought made me clench my fists so hard that my fingernails dug into my palm leaving bloody imprints. I was so emotional, especially back then before the weight of time and responsibility largely suffocated my restlessness. I vowed to myself not to let Jacob get to me again, not to lose control, no matter what happened. I squinted my eyes hard—as if to force the goal into my head.

While I sat there in the basement, Grandpa came down the stairs and walked through the office door.

"Grandma tells me you shot her the bird . . ."

I nodded while looking at the floor.

"On the driveway…"

I nodded again.

"She tells me she slapped the holy hell out of you in the kitchen."

I nodded again, still looking down.

"Well, she's upstairs. Hands and knees up there cleanin' up red shit off the cabinets. She must have busted you pretty good."

"It's Kool-Aid, Gramps."

He laughed as only he could. "You left your mark on that room. Everyone will remember that slap and splatter." And Grandpa walked over and patted me on the back. He told me to try to get along better with Jacob and "keep my head."

Things repeated themselves over that year. So much that it was like living in a spin cycle. We were always together, Jacob and I, working the same dawn until dusk shift at the farm. Like too many familial relationships it was a forced shitshow that led to nowhere good. "Jacob and I" lit a neighbor's pasture on fire and caused some damage to property. "Jacob and I" wrecked a farm truck. "Jacob and I" were caught stealing money from Grandpa's wallet. "Jacob and I" stole beer from the fridge. There was always a lot more Jacob and a whole hell of a lot less of "I." Though "I" was guilty by association.

Jacob and I never got along. I came to realize we never would. Jacob was drawn to pain and fear like an insect to bright light. He loved giving titty twisters that left scars for years. When he was really feeling froggy, which was often, he forced me to slap box him until my gums bled. You could never ride as a passenger in anything Jacob was driving, be it a four-wheeler, a pickup truck, or a bike. He would push the envelope of safety right up to the edge of death until you were in tears and begging to "make it stop."

Grandma's prediction about Jacob always hung in the back of my mind like a guilty thought. One of Grandma's favorite sayings was that "everyone served a purpose." *Even Jacob.* She was especially fond of reiterating that statement when Jacob got into trouble. I watched him deteriorate over the years—violent arrests, a stolen car, an arson charge for burning down a hundred-thousand-dollar grain elevator "just for shits and giggles." Grandma kept saying "*everyone* serves a purpose. *Everyone.* Jacob slid so far into the abyss that even unconditional advocates like her began to wonder just what that purpose might be.

If there was a moment where Grandma realized Jacob would not be able to live a normal life, it was the pigs. That changed everything, that was it. Things went from dysfunctional to something more malevolent. It was the coup de grâce of Jacob's sanity.

Jacob and I had just finished watching a comic book flick on the TV in the basement. A hackneyed yawner where the super-villain tied the hero to a post. The villain filled a trench with gas, and spent the last scene flipping a book of matches open and closed over the ditch while saying vague shit like "*you think I wanted this,*" "*I'm a monster,*" and "*no one ever loved me.*" The movie was boring and formulaic. Nonetheless, Jacob had "the face" while he mentally recorded the scene.

A few weeks later, he did it.

Jacob and I were playing near the pigpen. Grandpa had nestled the pen underneath a trio of thousand-year-old oaks right near the water pump. These trees were the oldest in the country. Massive oaks that had trunks so thick they were twelve feet across the middle Grandpa said the oaks were old even when he was a little boy and his dad had nicknamed them Comanche, Cherokee, and Apache after the warrior Indian tribes.

These three oaks were the centerpiece of the farm. They were so enormous, even in 1880, that the original homesteaders built the house so they could look upon the trees. They towered over the countryside each of them was over 150 feet tall and just as wide. They were never trimmed so their lower branches, thick as sidewalks, reached all the way to the ground. It was a rite of passage to climb to the top of Comanche's tallest limb. We built a tree house about forty feet up, cupped by the branches of Apache like a father coddles a newborn babe.

As an adolescent, I read this short story from John Muir about riding out the fury of a thunderstorm in the peak of a tree. I climbed up Comanche in the middle of a prairie deluge. The branches dipped thirty feet in high winds. I clung to the trunk, my eyes glued to the horizon as lightening carpet-bombed the chalky hills along the Smoky River in an awesome show. Hugging that tree, I felt the power of nature and the delicateness of life at the same time.

I know this sounds clichéd and sophomoric. With my ear to the trunk of Comanche, I heard the call. It was the most invigorating experience of my life and lit a fire inside me I could never extinguish. I loved that tree since that day.

One summer, Comanche, Cherokee, and Apache started to die. They got an unknown disease that caused their leaves to fall off in the middle of summer. It happened fast, in just two weeks. The hulking relics stood there bald and naked, with three feet of green leaves piled up around them. I still remember Grandpa standing to look at the trio stripped bare and dying during the height of the growing season. They had, at least according to Gramps, been there for well over "five hundred years." It was the end of an era that stretched longer from end to end than the American republic.

When those trees died, their leaves turned brown in a matter of days. The ground around the ancient trunks started to dry, and those poor pigs got hot. Even with the water pump dumping gallons of water onto the dirt, the ground began to flake and crack.

When Jacob dug his trench, that dirt was powder dry. He filled it with a line of red diesel. He stood over that trench for ten minutes, smoking a cigarette and flipping the box of matches open and closed.

"You think I give a fuck?" he said to me, imitating the supervillain from the movie with astounding skill.

He stared down into the box as if the answer was written in tiny letters along the side of a match. He finally pulled one and pinched it in his fingers, his eyes looking from the sulfur of the match-head to connect with mine. There was a flare in those eyes, a crazed glaze that was more akin to a rabid dog. He took a long draw off a cigarette he'd pilfered from Grandma. An inhale so deep, the smoke didn't even come out when he next spoke.

"Grandpa always loved you more. You're a soft little pussy. You'll hole up in the basement again. Eventually, he will come to pat you on the back."

He took another long pull, this time letting the smoke drift out of his mouth only to be pulled back in two long tusks of smoke. He made his right arm wiggle forward as if it had no bones. It swung like Dumbo's trunk. Only instead of a magic feather, there was a single wooden match.

"Ahhhhh," he said with genuine satisfaction, "He will lose his goddamned mind. You can try to explain it. Just try." He rubbed the back of his head with his palm and looked into the rolling hills of the pasture. Jacob had this look, kind of a contemplative stare into space where he'd raise his eyebrows and push out his chin. He would stay perfectly still while you looked at him. It was his I-am-a-deep-thinking-troubled-artist stare he probably bastardized from some B movie.

"I've enjoyed the pain," he said. "Do you know that?"

I didn't respond, that would have just made things worse.

Jacob lit the match then pinched it in his fingertips. His arm was completely extended. There was no bend in his elbow, Jacob let it burn slowly down without speaking. The flame of the match was, from my vantage point, perfectly between his eyes. Looking all the while past the flame at me.

"I love the fear—what's *crazy* Jacob going to do next? Fear lasts. It stays with people. And causing it, creating it… Ahhhhh God, it's the *best* feeling in the world."

The flame touched his hand then. His eyelids squinted, and there was a moment I could have stopped it, maybe redirected his attention away from that trench filled with diesel, away from those pigs. I only could muster a single word.

"Jacob…"

He dropped the match with a theatrical snap of his wrist. The diesel lit with a low, blue flame that crawled across the ground. It slithered into the pigpen with silent grace, and when its tendrils touched the drippings on the grates of the pen, it went up with a whoosh. The flames tore through the cage, rolling across the pink bellies of the piglets.

The sound that came from there was unlike anything I've heard before or since.

It was a squealing cough full of agony. The smell of burning hair and shit was so harsh I had to cover my nose with my shirt. The sound of those piglets choking themselves as they tried to push through the square grates as they burned alive. That sound never left my ears. Every time I smell a pork chop or hear the grunt of an animal, the memory of that day comes squealing back.

Above the din of the burning pigs, I could hear the trees begin to burn. Those ancient oaks swaying violently as their branches scratched together like antlers of bucks fighting to the death. I looked up, and the trees bent and bowed as they began to burn.

The fire stretched from the pigpen to the base of Comanche. The trunk browned then blacked and popped embers as the fire licked up its branches. In less than a minute, the flames had clawed its way to the top and spread to Apache and Cherokee. The fireball was the size of a New York skyscraper.

I didn't try to run. When Grandpa came, I offered no explanation. I just sat there, eyes wide, as Jacob smoked Indian-style and leered. A single pillar of black smoke stretched from the blaze ten thousand feet into the sky. It was as if the arm of the devil reached out of hell to claw hands at the heavens above.

The grandparents committed Jacob to a mental hospital the very next day. There was no goodbye, no explanation. Just a silent sendoff that served as an acknowledgment of their fear of Jacob. He had progressively gotten worse. He had gone from general physical abuse to vandalization to animal torture to full-scale slaughter. In this linear progression, animals wouldn't hold his attention much longer.

Looking back after all these years, I see that Grandma was right. Even a person as fuck-snap crazy as Jacob did have a purpose. There was a world where a kid that relished fear would have value. I didn't know it then, but that world—with its suffocating nights and roving killing herds—had started to develop all around me. The seeds of the apocalypse had just sprouted, and addled roots of the dead oaks had just broken through the soil.

CHAPTER TWO:

THE FACILITATOR

Robert Warrington's Journal
Token-Oak, Summer of 1996
8888 days before the Syndemic

I didn't see Jacob again for a long time. He spent two years committed at Shadow Mountain. They taught him, according to the grandparents, the "tools to cope." By the time Jacob got released, he was equipped to "handle the peaks and valleys of life." Unfortunately, those peaks were too high and those valleys too low.

I moved from Token-Oak to live with an Aunt Gina in the "big city" 300 miles away. Gina was a domineering woman who worked the night shift at a local hospital making beds and mopping floors. She lived in a mobile home nearby the hospital. Even though her house had four wheels and no yard, she kept it meticulously clean. No matter what the excuse, I was not to wake her from sleep. I spent my days tiptoeing around a rickety trailer barely grabbing door handles and plates just trying to survive. The only thing that didn't wake Gina was reading, so I devoured books on my twin bed at the end of the trailer.

Aunt Gina and I visited Token-Oak on holidays, and even that became rare. The grandparents sent me cards on birthdays, and we had the occasional phone call filled with the truncated dialectic between the elderly and children: "[question]: how was [blank]" . . . "[answer]: it was good." About once a year, the grandparents would visit. Most of the news I heard about Jacob was cliched mundanities about how he was "finding his way" or "the Lord's plan for him is different."

It wasn't until I was in high school that I saw Jacob again for any meaningful stretch. I'd bought my first car and itched to take my first trip. Vegas was out of the question. Even a day trip to the Lake of the Ozarks made my aunt nervous. Eventually, she agreed to let me stay with family. One summer morning, I loaded up my car and headed back.

Token-Oak had been calling me home ever since I left. On the drive back—my teenage nervousness with driving on the highway in full bloom—I thought about all the things I hated about the place: the smallminded bigotry of the town, the anger everyone seemed to wear around their neck like 7,000 scarves, and those fucking oak trees, dying everywhere. The broken fingers of their limbs reaching up into the sky like the tiny fingers of long-dead children. Most of all, though, I thought about that man on the driveway. I'd had dreams about his black gums for years. Waking up sweating, breathing in short puffs to avoid the ammonia stench, I'd curse the thought of Token-Oak.

I had to see it again. I had to.

Jacob was living in a dilapidated home on the south side of town. As Token-Oak's first neighborhood, Old Town houses were built at the turn of the nineteenth century. Big houses with sprawling lawns, there was a time when well-to-do citizens lived in Old Town. In 1955, the tire plant was built nearby, and a smoky haze blanketed the area. A few years later, an oil drilling company bought a plot of land across the road from the tire plant. All through the night, the clanging of pipes and the smell of burning rubber filled the air. Families left nice cape cods and Tudor homes to flee the nuisance. Over the years, Old Town buildings and homes turned black from the smoke. Rough necks and immigrants working nearby filled the neighborhood.

Jacob bought a home there, an L-shaped two-story in between a flop house for illegals and a home with all the glass broken out and no front door.

I met Jacob one Saturday, and he was raving about his new business on the outskirts of town. The tires of his new pickup thumped as we drove over railroad tracks into a neighborhood with single room cinderblock houses. A few of the houses were ashen-black with burnt roofs and shattered windows. Many others sat abandoned like open sores on a very sick patient. The lawns were dust patches littered with trash and dilapidated automobiles. Front doors of many of the houses sat wide open like amazed faces. The smell of ether singed the air.

A pregnant dog with enlarged teats darted out of a leafless bush. As we rolled through, I felt suspicious and alert and nostalgic at the same time.

At the edge of this neighborhood, there was an aluminum building with a steel door. It was surrounded by a ten-foot razor wire fence with a remote gate. In the back of the building, there was a garage door with two commercial padlocks. White gravel was thickly spread throughout the storefront. On a long, skinny piece of plywood, a sign outside hung under the peak of the roof that read "BUY, SELL, AND TRADE." It was an old-style sign, a pure anachronism that should have read "general store" or "saloon." The remote gate slid open, and Jacob and I pulled inside.

"What is this? A pawnshop?" I said, looking up at the sign.

"*Better*," Jacob said, striding to the entrance.

He pulled out a ring of keys and plucked one from a set of two dozen. After inserting the keys in the lock, he looked left and right then leaned to glance around the back of the building. He raised his eyebrows when he saw me watching him "C'est la vie," he said. When the door opened, he turned off an alarm near the front and hit several switches of lights. There was a large sign at the entrance that read "NO MORE THAN EIGHT PEOPLE IN THE STORE AT A TIME" in block letters.

The store had shelves on every wall. On each, as best I could tell, sat jugs, glass pitchers, rubber tubing, and all kinds of chemicals. The wares displayed were a mixture of garden supply store, indoor pool cleaning agents, and farming chemicals. In the far corner, there were generators of various sizes. In the back, there were two, 2,000-gallon trailers marked with anhydrous ammonia.

There were no prices listed on any item.

As I walked around the store, Jacob stepped behind the counter and pulled up a bar stool. He smiled while nodding his head. He spread his arms and swept the shop with his eyes. After a deep breath, he blew it out like a puff off a $50 cigar. He pulled out from behind the counter a double-barreled shotgun. He broke the gun open, looked in the barrels, confirmed it was loaded then snapped it shut.

"You know what it is now?" Jacob said, standing.

"It's a store for chemicals?" I said.

"Am I going to have to spell it out for you?"

"He touched a shelf near the door that had smaller bottles and batteries. "You got your lower rung shake and bake stuff here." He stepped a few feet to the right next to matches and a series of plastic jugs and tubes. "Here is your Nazi Cold/P2P cook." He stepped back a little further to a steel tank and near the generators. "I can even provide the necessaries for an industrial cook. Top quality shit, too." And he banged a 500-gallon steel drum that reverberated through the room in a loud wobble.

"You can *legally* do this?" I said.

"What's illegal here? Name one thing. Hell, I am even a licensed dealer for the fertilizer. Check the name on the jeans, broseph! That says it all." He pointed to the back of his jeans at the Levi's logo.

Jacob told me about his hero: Levi Strauss. During the 1849 California gold rush, hundreds of thousands of miners hit the hills and streams of rural Cali looking to strike it rich. Only a few of them found gold and fewer still made money. Most ended up broke, desperate, and dead in pursuit of the dream. But "Uncle Levi" was a visionary, instead of focusing on the unlikely profits, he outfitted gold rushers with new pants, double stitched with denim fabric. He made a killing, and his empire grew, according to Jacob, by "feeding the frenzy."

"Sutter's Mill is now in shambles. But Levi's has a corporate headquarters on the San Fran pier that ships clothes worldwide."

"So, you're outfitting the meth crisis?"

"Nah. *I'm a facilitator,*" Jacob said as he grabbed the shotgun on the counter and rested it on his hip. Jacob was posturing again, and the message he wanted to convey was clear: he was not to be fucked with. He explained his profit margins and how he tipped the police to "unusual purchases" so they never gave him any trouble. There was a specific dealer, a "skinhead with a bridge piercing and facial tattoo" that bought over half his supplies each month and paid for information about any new cooks.

"Who is this guy?" I asked.

"He is quiet—comes late—after dark. He pulls his truck in the garage and takes a tank of anhydrous and some parts. Pays cash and asks who's cooking. Some weeks, I make three or four thousand off of him alone."

"Four thousand... in a week?"

Jacob laughed and slapped the counter.

Jacob walked to the window and pulled the string on a neon open sign. He pressed a button to open the front gate. A razor wire chain link on wheels rattled backward. Jacob walked back to the barstool on the counter and sat down with his shotgun within reach. "Watch this," he said with a wry smile. In less than ten minutes, the place was filling up with "customers."

The first person to shuffle in was a woman in her mid-thirties. She had wild, red hair and her freckled skin was pockmarked with sores. The skin on her face sagged in flabby pouches so I could see the outline of her skull. She blinked often and hard. A blue T-shirt that had holes across the belly had a picture of a grey wolf. It took me a while to realize that these were cigarette burns.

Her focus was in the shake and bake section. She picked up a two-liter bottle and a few packages of batteries. She shuffled to the counter, set them down, and stepped back with her eyes on the floor.

"Fifty," Jacob said, staring a hole through the woman.

She pulled out a fifty, slid it across the counter, and picked up her supplies. She shuffled out the shop without making a sound. There was a rhythm to purchasing materials from the store, and she knew it well. In less than a minute, she disappeared between two houses.

"You see that?" Jacob said, smiling. "That's respect. First time, she gave me trouble. But I put that shit down quick."

"Fifty for a bottle and two batteries? That's crazy."

"Yeah," he said through a pride-filled smile. "She's going back to her house to start a batch in her little bottle. In a few hours, she'll have a thousand dollars' worth of "dirty meth." He said she was a "small-timer," but a steady customer. "In a way, she's smart," he said. "She does *just* enough to avoid being tracked by the cops or put down by the big timers."

A few minutes later, the shop filled up with more customers. Several of which looked like they were in high school. They were looking in the "Nazi Cold" area. One of them, a kid with a backward cap and skinny jeans below his waist, picked up a jug and some tubing and brought them to the counter.

He leaned in close to Jacob and said in a suggestive whisper, "So . . . I need heat to break down pseudo or can I do it cold?"

Jacob's face contorted into a snarl so intense his eyebrows covered half of his eyes. The kid stepped back and exchanged a glance with his friends. This question, it was clear, was not part of the well-established shop etiquette. Jacob reached up and grabbed the materials from the kid's hands. He set them behind the counter. And walked around and seized the kid by the shoulder.

"Get the fuck out of here. I don't know what you think, but we don't do that here."

I saw then that Jacob had indeed matured into a man. It wasn't a display of force—I have no doubt he would have hit that kid if necessary—it was the fact he showed calculated restraint in handling the situation.

Jacob watched them all leave. He sat back down and explained that high schoolers just getting into the trade often wandered in the store. He did not allow store customers to discuss the making of meth inside—"no synthesis talk, no exceptions." Most importantly, he explained, he did not make scenes with the kids. According to Jacob, they had "parents, people that cared." A corollary to the rule, Jacob treated full-blown addicts differently.

A man walked in wearing a dirty wife-beater and itching at a ragged beard. There was an instant tension when he entered the shop. His eyes were glazed, and his fat tongue bulged in his mouth. He looked fifty but had the bouncy movements of a younger man. The skin on his arms hung in flabby rivulets riddled with acne. He had a tattoo, an Aztec chieftain astride a pyramid of skulls, with bold lettering, the phrase "Aztlán" coiling up one arm to the base of his chin. There were seven black teardrops tattooed on a single cheek. His eyes connected with the two tanks near the back of the store and he shifted in that direction.

Jacob saw the man walk past and stood behind the counter and scowled.

"Those are ag only!" Jacob said loud enough to grab everyone's attention. The man stopped and looked Jacob up and down. Two tweakers near the door slipped out. Another customer froze and started shaking. I noticed a bulge in the man's belt at the base of his spine. When he turned to square up with Jacob, I saw it was a gun. Guns tell the truth. You can tell a person's experience with firearms by the way they walk. This man had been carrying for a long time.

I held my breath as I stepped back from the counter towards the back of the store. My nerves took over, and my knees shook.

The man smiled at Jacob, exposing a row of golden teeth.

"Necessito… fifty gallons," the man said in Spanish accent.

"Motherfucker, *that's AG-RI-CUL-TUR-AL only*." Jacob's hands reached under the counter and his fingers wrapped around a shotgun.

The man looked at the tanks and back at Jacob. There was a stillness in the room as the man's eyes danced over the store. There was a calculus occurring in his head. When he reached the end of his conclusion, he chuckled. I heard confidence in that laugh, a sound that said he had no problems putting blood on the floor.

He reached behind his back while exposing his horsey teeth.

I hoped to make it to the back of the store, but I knocked into a pallet of aluminum cans, sending them crashing to the cement floor.

An electric snap of a tazer vibrated through the room. There was a hollow moan that mimicked the sound of the electric current. The man grabbed his chest while going down to one knee. Jacob jumped the counter with his shotgun, landing with both feet. Raising the butt of the shotgun, Jacob struck the man in the face with the butt of the gun. He caught him clean on the right cheek. The bone-chilling sound of cracking teeth preceded another moan.

The man collapsed backward clutching his face. Jacob pulled the handgun from behind the man's back and pistol-whipped the man across the forehead. The sound of metal smacking a skull bone produced a dull "*thwap*." The man balled up on the floor in exquisite pain. The man's desperate hands grabbed the handgun and Jacob pinned his wrist to the concrete.

"Let it go!" Jacob commanded. But the man, even on his back, was defiant. He held on. He clenched his teeth and glared up at Jacob, who towered over him with the shotgun.

"*Libre Soy*!" Jacob said. Jacob aimed the shotgun at the soft part of the man's throat.

36

The man spat through cracked lips. Blood ran down his forehead and across his face. He pulled himself up, as far as he could with his wrist still pinned, and screamed, "*jódete hijo de puta!*"

Jacob took the butt of the shotgun and brought it down on the man's knuckles. I heard the man's bones breaking against the floor. The man screamed, and Jacob shoved the barrel of the shotgun several inches down his throat. The gun barrel separated more teeth as it destroyed the man's tonsils. There was a desperate gasp of air as the man took sharp breaths through his nose. Blood covered his face and neck. Each breath was a hollow gargle. In less than thirty seconds, Jacob had obliterated the man's face.

Jacob grabbed the pistol off the pavement. He slid it into the pocket of his pants. Jacob released the man's wrist. The broken fingers of the man's hand contorted into directions in which they were not meant to turn. Jacob leaned into the butt of the shotgun pressing it into the man's tonsils and cracked teeth. The tearing flesh caused the man to whistle a muffled howl through the gun barrel. It reminded me of how we used to blow on the bottles of our soda pops as a kid. Jacob held the gun in that position until the man was entirely out of breath. Jacob pulled the shotgun free, the barrel dripped a river of blood and mucus on the floor. Jacob raised the dripping barrel and pointed it directly at the man's head.

There was a calmness to Jacob, though he held an intense stare. His fingers tightened over the trigger as his lips stretched over his teeth.

The man rolled to his stomach and broke into a run. He hit the steel door of the entrance so hard he tumbled to the ground in the white gravel outside. In his wake, he left a bloody trail through the shop and on the door.

Two customers stood silent, watching Jacob. Their mouths agape in shock.

I could not stop shaking. I crouched in the corner surrounded with aluminum cans. I had come so close to death. One wrong move, one fumble of the finger—hell, an unexpected sneeze—and that could have gone much differently. I forced myself to breathe in through my mouth and out my nose, counting each inhale. One . . . ahhh . . . two . . . ahhh.

Jacob walked over and handed me a spray bottle. "Calm down," he said and asked me to clean the blood from the floor and on the door. Before I could refuse, he pulled out his cell phone and stepped past me to the back of the shop by the anhydrous tanks. He spoke in a hushed tone into his iPhone.

"The Mexicans are back."

The voice on the other end asked a question that I heard vaguely mumbled.

"Guy's wearing a beater—face all smashed to shit—driving a Black Silverado heading south on MLK." There was a short pause as Jacob looked up front. He mumbled something into the phone and stuffed it back into his pocket.

Jacob took the spray bottle from me and asked me to sit behind the counter. He cleaned up the blood on the floor and the walls quickly. Bleaching it and then soaking it up with a mop. He brought in a leaf blower and had everything dry in a few minutes. He had a system for cleaning up such a mess and the tools at the ready. The store never shut down, even for a minute.

I sat inside watching customers for another two hours, focusing on my breathing. During that time, over fifty people wandered in. The clear majority of them were full-blown addicts and cooks. They overpaid for parts without a word. Throwing down twenties and fifties for things they could buy from Walmart—which Token-Oak did not have—for a tenth of the price.

Jacob didn't speak again until late afternoon. The customers shuffled silently about. The shop filled up, there were people in front of every shelf, perhaps eight, maybe ten. All were veterans of the trade. One more walked in, and Jacob stood. He refused to let an additional person in the store and kicked one more out.

In that day alone, Jacob netted over $2500. By five, he locked the front door, padlocked the garage, and we drove out of the gate. He had this little grin on his face, a quiet satisfaction as he turned the wheel, guiding his truck back across the railroad tracks. We turned south on MLK.

As we drove over the bridge into Old Town, Jacob looked over to the passenger seat and said, "It's not for everyone."

"It's not for me," I said, still rattled from the incident. Jacob laughed and whistled to the radio. "You beat the hell out of that guy. Once he sobers up… heals up, he'll come back."

Jacob cocked his head to the side and looked over at me with a toothy grin. There was something he understood behind that smile, something he would not share. He turned the wheel and took a deep breath.

"He won't."

I thought about asking more questions, but I let it slide. It was one of those feelings people get, perhaps a conversational cue. I didn't want to know more, so it sat. And we drove down Main Street listening to the radio as we headed towards Jacob's home.

"Why only eight?"

"Huh?" Jacob said in response. "Eight what?"

"In the shop, why do you cap it at eight people? There is enough room."

Jacob explained that, for whatever reason, once the shop filled up with over eight tweakers, they displayed unusual behavior. They seemed more standoffish. He felt they were "doglike" and when they "packed up" they felt fearless. So, he kept the number of customers searching the shop small at eight.

Once we arrived at Jacob's house, we walked upstairs. He said he wanted to "show me something I'd appreciate." We climbed out a second-story window onto an old shake shingle roof. And we laid on our backs in between two half-dead oak trees looking across the rooftops of Token-Oak. The sun set behind the buildings of downtown. Jacob lit up a joint as he looked out across the quaint tableau of the small town. He took a long draw while watching the fading daylight for a long time. It wasn't comfortable, not exactly, because there were no comfortable moments with Jacob, but it was a pause in the madness.

Token-Oak, like so many small towns, was built around a courthouse. The building had four columns and a clock tower at its apex. Though not the tallest building in town, it was the most commanding. Blazing white and set upon a slight hill for all to see, the courthouse evoked a Grecian heritage.

In the center of the courthouse square, there was the Token-Oak. The old oak had a way of making people stop in mid-stride to take in its twisting branches. They say that the beautiful old oak on the hill was the reason the first settlers stopped in the town. The pioneers named the village after the tree, viewing its strong trunk and vast branches as emblematic of the town's inevitable future success; a "token" of good times that were sure to follow. Every town event dating back to the 1860s was held under its branches. For a hundred and fifty years, the "token oak" symbolized manifest destiny and the rugged frontier spirit of its founders.

"It's dying," Jacob said. "The Token-Oak. It started dropping leaves last year, and they say they are going to leave it alone."

We both looked out at the old tree for several minutes.

Set off from the high school, there was a football field with enough stadium lights surrounding it that gave it an ethereal feel. At night, the field glowed as a bubble of brilliant light. It made you understand the fascination so many youths had with the game.

On the outskirts, north of town, there was the meat packing plant surrounded by feedlots of soon-to-be slaughtered cows. Nearly every night, you could hear the wailing of the herd, and if you really listened, you could feel the cattle calling to those headed into the plant. Those yearning bawls were Token-Oak's background noise

Far in the distance, about two miles northeast, some hills rolled together into each other leaving deep ruts. The view of the setting sun above those hills with the bright clouds just above was spectacular. The townspeople called these deep roots the Hollows. The forest of oaks surrounding Token-Oak was exceptionally thick, but it was a veritable riot of tangled branches along the Hollows. So thick, that some claimed, sunlight couldn't touch the ground.

The dark lines of the Hollows meandered to a rare bald spot on the tallest hill in the county. People called this bald spot the Hilltop. The Hilltop held a macabre lore that never lost its power to scare. Back in the day, it was rumored that Osage Indians used to come from all over America to die up there. They would sit Indian-style and pile fist-sized rocks in a ring around their legs and let the elements do the rest. They were sick or old or just too sad to live anymore. They would die out in the open, sitting upright enclosed by the rock circles. And the sun and the wind would dry their skin tight, and the skeleton would stay upright in that position for months. The Osage believed the Hilltop was a conduit to the dead. A rally point for the living to meet with deceased loved ones.

There were hundreds of rock circles sitting up there undisturbed. And they weren't all old-school circles, either. Every year, a teenager, a mother who lost her daughter to a drunk driving accident, a depressed middle-aged man, walked into the dark of the Hollows and up to the Hilltop. They sat down in a circle of rocks and "died." Anyone who went into those woods, townsfolk said, rarely came back. If they did, they were different, disconnected from their family and friends, they might wander the town for a time, but they eventually disappeared. That fact, more than the weird stories, prevented people from fucking around up there.

The Hollows were full of off-the-grid types and had its share of meth labs and murders. Supposedly, a collective of dealers and ne'er-do-wells ran the Hollows. No one went into the Hollows for a stroll. At the crossing of two dirt roads at the base of the Hollows, someone had been dumping dead town dogs there for as long as I could remember. It was a message, a not-so-subtle reminder to anyone that might wander into the dead oaks. It worked, too. Few went in those woods. Not even the cops. Unless they were going to drag out a body. Even then, they walked in at noon, eight deep, fully loaded.

To Jacob and me, the Hollows held a nervous fascination. It was more legend than story. There were town kids that claimed to have a circle rock from the Hilltop that would whisper to them at night. Every few months, there was a fire lit in the darkness of the Hilltop. I knew a kid with a telescope who claimed to see pagan-style dancing around the fire. Everyone had a story from McClintock's Tree Farm claiming to see lines of people in the woods. When the wind blew in from the Northeast, which was rare, a haze drifted into town that reeked like ether. There were bits of truth braided with exaggeration, yet the Hollows were real enough. It was the one thing that Jacob was scared to face.

Jacob had been trying to get me to go to the Hilltop since we were little kids. But it held such a mystical fear that we never made the trip.

We sat on the shake shingles of his roof, staring at the Hilltop. As the sun was setting, the ring of the horizon—especially north of town—was dotted with eighty-foot-tall oil rigs. Each one lit up in the shape of a Christmas tree. It gave the little town a bustling feel.

As I looked over at Jacob, he was doing it again. That weird ass thing he did when he knew people were watching him. It was his "deep-thinking-stare" and he was looking right at the Hilltop.

"We should go tonight," Jacob whispered.

I took a long pull of my beer and shook my head in the negative.

"*We should,*" he said again with more force, but still no real motivation.

"People don't come back," I said in quick response.

"That is bullshit. That lady came back. The teacher with the two twin girls. What was her name? Amanda something."

"She came back for two weeks. Remember? And she got a motel room and didn't speak to a single person. Not even her kids. A few people saw her around town. She was all freaked out. Right before she disappeared. And her family moved away a few weeks later."

"Well, the point is, she came back."

I laughed at this, and we both looked up at the Hilltop. An October wind was blowing across town. A dust devil spun leaves along the ditches of MLK.

"We could sneak in from the north. That old creek bed that runs through Miller's pasture. It's low and dry and rounds straight up to the Hilltop. Come on, Bha-*aab*. It'll be fun. For old times' sake?

That nickname. I hadn't heard it in years and, hearing it now, it brought back all the old insecurities. For the briefest of moments, I had relaxed with Jacob. That silly moniker wrecked any rapport that was building. I realized, looking at Jacob, that he was waiting for the right moment to insert the jab. It was the first of many insults, I was sure. I let it pass.

Jacob took a quick pull of his beer and emptied the longneck. He threw it off his roof in a twisting parabola over the reaching fingers of the dead oaks. The bottle hit the street below and shattered.

Old Town was full of older homes with big porches. Jacob's immediate neighbor had couches in the front yard. Another had two bumper pull campers sitting on blocks with an extension cord running to each. The house across the street had a hole in a wall the exact size of a car. It was the kind of neighborhood where breaking glass bottles was an everyday occurrence.

"You think that's true? You think a person can talk to the dead?" he said, looking at me with squinted eyes.

I didn't answer. We both stared out across Token-Oak. Out through the dead branches of the trees near his house. I heard the bawling of the cattle as they shuffled into the slaughterhouse plant. Faint cries floated on the wind. Just to the North, I saw roughnecks on oil rigs twisting pipe thousands of feet down into the earth. Each pipe spinning into the liquefied remains of ancient life buried beneath eons of geology.

It was a Friday night, a half mile away the football stadium was glowing. There was a helmet crack, and Jacob and I listened to the roar of the crowd. From such a distance, it sounded like an exasperated moan that twisted into the night.

Courthouse square was bathed in brilliant moonlight. A twisting string of low-lying clouds floated above. It was a beautiful side view of the town. From the third story of Jacob's roof, you could see about everything: the Elks Lodge, McGuillicuddy Mortuary, Zion Lutheran Church, and the open ground around the massive white columns of the courthouse. You could even see the alleys between the principal streets of the town.

I took a long pull on my beer. It was my fifth, and I felt a little loose. So, I threw it in the same spinning parabola that Jacob had. I tossed it a little too hard, and a rictus of alley cats erupted as the glass of my longneck shattered below. Jacob looked at me in a broad smile, though his lips never parted. He was well past five beers, and it showed.

Suddenly, he was up on his elbows looking out at the courthouse square. His eyes narrowed, and his mouth opened in a perfect circle. He raised his index finger to point out. "Watch this," he said.

There were people on every corner of the courthouse square. All of them standing in front of back alleys. The sun dipped below the horizon, and I didn't remember seeing so many people moments before. But I didn't know. I was sixteen and drinking longnecks on a roof. It wasn't my best moment for memory.

"Who are those people?" I said, looking at Jacob. Token-Oak had several dozen town drunks that wobbled around at night. Shuffling between two dive bars on opposite sides of the courthouse like seasonal birds. They hit the Elks for happy hour, the Moose Bar for quarter beers, and then migrated to McSmitty's Bar (a local dive named for its owner, so the drunks called it McShitty's bar) for closing time. It wasn't uncommon to see a few drunks slouching about. But looking out at the square that night, there were at least two dozen. All of them stumbling around.

"Tweakers," Jacob said, "Now watch."

Jacob had gone from leaning on his elbows to sitting, to a full stand as he looked out on the town. He was moving his index finger and mouthing numbers with a Shiner Bock still in one hand.

"Twenty-nine," he said without looking at me. "And there is another one by McGuillicuddy's and the cemetery, so thirty."

"Twenty-nine?"

"Thirty," Jacob said, correcting me. ". . . wait for it . . ."

They were all moving in various directions, at least it seemed that way at first, but as I stared out, I saw something unique. All thirty took a step at the same time, in a weird shimmy. They moved a quarter block in a few seconds, each of them with curled hands and their necks contorted way to the left. We were too far away, but I swore it looked like their teeth were shut, yet their lips curled back. They walked a few more gamboling steps. Then, as if on a cue, all thirty did the same thing again.

"Whoa . . ." I said raising to a stand, "that is fucking spooky."

In a few seconds, most were blocked by our vantage point and disappeared behind buildings. In a few more, they were all gone, as quickly as they came.

He only nodded. "This place is full of surprises."

And he sat and glared out at the square for at least an hour. A few groups of people wandered underneath the Token-Oak in the square. There was a rowdy group of town kids smashing pumpkins. We watched the cops give a half dozen sobriety test to patrons leaving the Elks. But the tweakers didn't come back. Not that night, at least.

CHAPTER THREE:

THE BURNING OF THE OLD VICTORIAN

Robert Warrington's Journal
Token-Oak, Summer of 1996
8887 days before the Syndemic

We crawled in off the roof around one a.m. Jacob's home was quite a palace during the Hoover Administration, with three floors and hardwoods throughout. In spots, the walls of the home shifted outward. The plaster ceilings broke into small pieces when I walked by. The water that came from rattling pipes was rust colored. There were birds in the attic, and I heard their clawed feet scratch above. A red fungus spread from water spots in the corners of the room in fuzzy circles that were so virulent there were white flower pods in places.

That night, I slept upstairs in the guest bedroom. Jacob used the room to store oil paintings he was "working on." His pieces were psychedelic, the kind of art admired by teenage potheads. Pastel-colored skulls with joints hanging out, they looked like they were purchased at a headshop. His more artsy pieces—landscapes and pictures of fruit—were clipped from an art history book sitting open on an easel in the corner. Jacob was an imitator and good at making copies.

Around 3:00 a.m., I passed out on a sheetless mattress while staring at a rough copy of Van Gogh's self-portrait. Fitful sleep—I tottered somewhere between stoned and blackout drunk—shook me for a few hours. In the early morning hours, my bladder ached, and I rose to use the bathroom. Unfamiliar with the house, I fumbled through the darkness, arms extended. The hallway was uneven, and the upstairs had shag carpet that grabbed toes in its tangles. I kept my head down and focused on unsure steps. It took me twenty minutes to find my way back to my mattress.

That night, I heard creaking floorboards. Someone walked down the staircase, through the living room, and out the back door. Century-old wood slats filled with dust announced the sound of any step in the house like a dozen out-of-tune violins. The moon was full, and the white light illuminated my room.

I heard the subtle hum of a large engine from the driveway. Muffled voices came from somewhere in the darkness below outside my window.

I rose from my bed and looked out. Just past the porch, I saw a ten-foot long black pearl hood. It stretched on and on, fronted by a pair of retractable headlamps and a chrome grill. I was gazing upon a Lincoln Continental Mark III. Maybe a 1979 or 1980. The brontosaurus of cars. By far the largest of its kind from an extinct species. The car was a black pearl with whitewall tires and an upholstered roof. It glimmered in the night like the skin of a great white. The old Lincolns hailed from the age of spacious designs with comically long hoods and couch-like interior seating. I'd always respected that old-school style.

Next to the vehicle, there was a bald man that towered over Jacob. He wore a tank top that was stretched to its absolute limit. His shoulders were three feet across, and the man had a tattoo that ran up his spine; the outline of the hilt and blade of a flaming broadsword. There were three subdermal implants on the sides of his head that looked like horns about to break through the skin. Bathed in the moonlight, the man shimmered, his bald reflected the light.

The skinhead had a sheet of paper in his fingers. He handed it over to Jacob.

There was something in Jacob's posture I had never seen. Jacob's head ducked, and his shoulders slumped over. He held his hands cupped in a non-threatening gesture. The man spoke, and Jacob nodded. But Jacob never said a word, and he kept his eyes on the ground. I realized Jacob was cut two ways: he deeply respected this man and was terrified by his presence. God, I thought, what would it take to scare Jacob like that. I moved closer to the window, pressing my face into a corner to hear better.

Their backs were turned toward me as the man pointed to the paper. He handed Jacob an envelope and a burlap sack. Jacob stuffed the envelope in his back pocket and grabbed the bag. The contents of the sack looked heavy as Jacob grabbed it firmly with both hands and immediately set it down. Whatever was inside made a loud clacking sound as they settled on the concrete. The man looked Jacob in the face and punctuated the air with his hand. In a voice so deep, it sounded like a bass drum, the man said "daytime" so "people can see." The man's voice sounded like a harsh whisper that carried well on the night air. Jacob nodded several times and looked back down.

The skinhead took a step towards the old Lincoln. Once he reached the hood, he stopped and stood still. It was a whole-body pause like he felt something unusual. He looked up at the moon and took in a deep breath. For no reason at all—I had not moved or made a sound, I don't even think I blinked—the man snapped his head back towards the window where I knelt. His eyebrows pinched inward, and his massive jaw shook. His face was a snarl.

My face was in the darkness of the room, but the tips of my fingers rested on the window sill in the moonlight. The man twisted his left hand with his palm facing up. He raised his arm as he closed all his fingers into a fist. I felt a pain, an intense burning, in my fingertips that were exposed to the moonlight. There was a hissing inside my head, an alien pocket of sound like pool water stuck in an ear. The hiss melded into a whisper and then grew into a scream. I saw the eyes of that man then, pupils the size of silver dollars staring back at me. For the briefest of moments, I felt that skinhead's hand inside my skull. The massive fingers twisting into the grey matter of my brain. And the thought crossed my mind to hurl myself through the glass onto the broken boarded porch below. I felt pulled against my will.

The moonlight on my skin warmed. It felt like a bad sunburn then it singed like I'd touched a hot pan. The tiny hairs on my knuckles curled and dissolved in the heat. The skinhead glared into the window, his fist shaking violently.

I yanked my fingers out of the moonlight and dove back to the bed I slept on. I closed my eyes and listened, taking quiet breaths. If the man came into the house, I'd hear him on the wood. I sat in silence waiting for footsteps. My heart thumped as my ears strained in the darkness.

After thirty seconds, I heard the car door open followed by the rumbling of an engine. The car rumbled away into the darkness, the pistons thumping down the black streets of Old Town. I raised my head to look out the window. The taillights of the old Lincoln shone on the cracked asphalt underneath a canopy of ancient oaks.

There was something behind the car. At first, I thought it was just a feeling, a remnant of fear radiated off the skinhead. But it instantly became more. Old Town had come to life. Entire pockets of shadows slithered in the wake of the black-pearl Lincoln Mark III. The streets subtly moved in the wake of the car. All the while, I heard a low whistle. A thick, hollow sound that issued from the Lincoln.

In a few seconds, in the wake of that car, there were dozens of "people." In a half minute, I saw a hundred. All shuffling towards the Lincoln's taillights. It was an itchy crowd, ill-clothed and dirty, that stammered in the awkward steps of an addict stoned to the gills.

For the first time, I saw the scope of Token-Oak's meth problem. It was a scourge, a living, breathing entity of addicts spilling out into the moonlight. I'd seen drugs before, and occasionally, I'd felt awkward in a town convenience store when a full-blown meth head twitched in to buy a lighter and cigarettes. But this… holy shit, it was something else.

They were everywhere: spilling out of porches, underneath spreading branches of dying oaks, in gutters, and stumbling down driveways. That hollow whistle beckoned them into the darkness. The thought occurred, what if this problem, this epidemic, was in other towns, too? The whole goddamn country would collapse.

That night, I watched the addicts shuffle until 4:30 in the morning. Eventually, exhaustion drove me back to the sheetless mattress. I had a fitful rest, always thinking about the scene just outside. The eyes of that skinhead in the moonlight haunted my thoughts. Like hell itself was only a thin sheet of glass or a few squealing wooden steps from my throat.

Jacob woke me up around seven. He yanked the pillow from underneath my head. "Shithead," he said, "we're headed to breakfast. We piled into Jacob's Buick LeSabre and drove to the local Tasty Freeze to get sausage biscuits.

I ordered from the drive-through window. The coffee was too hot to drink. I blew through the hole in the lid and took short sips. Jacob drove around Token-Oak eating hash brown discs out of a cardboard box. He turned the LeSabre down MLK across from the winding sidewalks of the local park. I leaned against the window as Token-Oak slid past.

Jacob was in a musical kind of mood. I could tell something was up. He had this weird habit of whistling during awkward moments. Not just any tune, a Civil War song, performed with the panache of a contestant in an elimination round. Jacob continued as he guided the LeSabre into a parking space along MLK across from the basketball courts at the edge of the Token-Oak City Park.

People were stretched-out on blankets on the park lawn looking at the trees. The meandering Smokey River wiggled through thickets of some ancient oaks. There were sets of hardwoods on both sides of the river that touched over the water like a covered bridge. Giant trunks, thick as the columns at the Pantheon and just as straight, these trees that got fat and happy drinking from the river bed. The county had built stone bridges across the river out a square where the city maintained a rose garden. As far as Token-Oak went, it was a beautiful place. People got married there, had graduation ceremonies, and, every year, the site hosted Oktoberfest. There was a brewing competition that drew contestants from six counties. People prepared for Oktoberfest in a panicked frenzy, like Londoners shuffling about just before the Luftwaffe night bombings.

I had been to that park hundreds of times. I knew every tree, bridge, and crossing like a blind person knows the outlay of their living room furniture. There was something different this time, the park had an exposed feel. As we parked, the sun fell on the river and the rose garden, usually a place of shade covered solace. Along the river, the massive oaks were leafless and dead even though it was the middle of summer. Strips of bark fell off those dead trees in halfpipe sheaves. There were owl holes in the trunks and broken branches on the ground. Sadness settled over me, and I realized that I'd thought those trees were eternal.

"Damn," I said with my face up to the window, surveying the damage, "what happened to the park?"

Jacob positioned the old Buick into a different parking space. He pulled forward a little, maneuvering the car to get a better view of both the basketball courts and down Main Street. It was difficult to find the right spot because the High Rise was in the way. Finally, he settled on a spot that allowed him to see both.

"The trees," I said a little louder, irritated that he did not respond.

"*It's a damn shame,*" he said in response, though his tone indicated that he didn't care. He just kept whistling, and he looked at the basketball courts.

"What are we doing here?" I said as the whistling intensified. I looked out and saw nothing.

"We're fixing something," Jacob said. A middle-aged woman wearing a jogging outfit walked two dogs, a bullmastiff, and a basset hound, through the park. The dogs sniffed spots along the park, both their tails wagging furiously. Their leashes hung slack as they ambled through the underbrush near Smokey River. Jacob eyed the woman until she turned along a new path leading the dogs along the sidewalk into the rose garden.

"Fixing what?" I said.

Jacob got out of the car and popped the trunk. He pulled out the burlap sack from the night before. Grasping the bag in his fist, he held it close to his leg as he walked across MLK into the park. His head darted in a nervous thither. Jacob moved under the trees towards a corner of the basketball courts.

The sun shined above in a cloudless sky, and the court teemed with ballers. There was an adult game on one side with a few spectators clutching the chain-link fence and sitting on balls. On the other half of the court, middle schoolers, perhaps a few grade schoolers, sprinted around. The younger game had dozens of kids around the court and a few more sitting on small aluminum bleachers.

I remembered the court from my childhood. With the police station right across the street, my grandma always encouraged me to go there. "There is not a safer spot in town," she always said. Cop shop or not, we still got into trouble. It was a place to make friends and pretend to smoke cigarettes. I saw my first nudie magazine on those bleachers and drank a sip of Kentucky

Deluxe by the creek. My third-grade best friend, Jonnie Terabaso, was an east coast transplant who'd regale us with stories of first kisses and failed pranks he pulled at school. I never laughed so hard in all my life. Seeing the kids play now, I missed those untainted moments, those childhood freedoms.

Jacob lurked through the rose garden with the burlap bag. When he was about a hundred yards from the court, he stopped suddenly underneath a thicket of trees near the park restroom. There was a water fountain a few feet away. Jacob let the burlap bag drop to the ground, and he pressed it underneath a shrub behind the fountain with his foot. The burlap sack disappeared under the bush. He was seamless with the drop. I didn't realize what he had done until he was halfway back to the car. He jumped in the Buick and kept his eyes on the ball court.

We sat there ten minutes, just looking out at the Token-Oak Park watching the kids play ball. The woman with dogs walked in a circuitous path up and down the Smokey. Their tails had stopped, and they skittishly searched the park. The basset hound was low to the ground, his muzzle sniffing. Jacob scrutinized everything, like a cop on a stakeout. All the while Jacob whistled "Swing Low Sweet Chariot." He belted out the lows at an agonizingly slow pace.

"That is annoying. Stop," I said.

He kept it up, staring at the kids. As he hit the notes, I started to fantasize about beating him. A quick throat punch, maybe a swift jab to the nuts. Jacob brought out the worst in people, and each of his whistles directed my anger like a conductor at a symphony. Right when I was about to snap, Jacob stopped cold.

He sat bolt upright with his fingertips resting on his thighs. He stopped breathing, and the muscles in his face and neck tightened.

I heard a sound on the air. Like music heard from far away, but I could barely make it out. My ears strained as I leaned in to decipher the whispered noise. Then I caught it, just the faintest of notes. It was a deep, hollow whistle as if the sound itself was swallowing a moan. Even in the daylight, the sound sent gooseflesh up my arms. I strained my neck turning my head in all directions searching for the long-hooded Lincoln.

"Do you hear that?" I said, not finding the car.

Jacob didn't answer. He didn't have to. His face was full of anticipation. So, I turned to the game. A new set of kids was on the court. These kids were ten, possibly twelve, judging by their height and the awkward way they shot the ball, still having to step into longer shots to reach the hoop. They ran like rabbits back and forth. The game was a free-for-all with no positions or strategy. A kid stole the ball, and all nine swarmed towards the other hoop. Crashing into the paint like they could do something when they closed on the rim. Another steal, and they'd swarm again. A mob of kids spinning and enveloping into itself. It was exhausting to watch.

There was a missed shot and a rebound. A sandy-blonde kid with quaffed hair grabbed the ball with both hands. A talented player, the kid easily dribbled while watching the court. As he reached the center of the court, he pulled up. His head tilted slightly to the left. There was an intense look on his face, but he wasn't looking at the game. He turned to look at the courthouse. For a moment, he stood perfectly still. Then the ball dropped from his hands and bounced on the asphalt. The swarm of kids folded around him crashing towards the bouncing ball. The sandy-blonde didn't respond. He stood there, oblivious like he was on another planet.

In the fracas near the basket, another kid stopped moving. He didn't have the ball, so he was harder to spot. He wore a ballcap with a college logo of a purple wildcat. His head had the same leftward tilt. As he stood, motionless, the game moved around him. The other kids followed the ball and failed to notice two players had stopped amid adolescent chaos.

The two kids, sandy-blonde and the ball cap, stood still, looking towards the courthouse. A brisk wind swept across the park and a swirl of autumn leaves spun in a tornadic spiral across the court. The sandy-blonde's quaffed hair blew in his face. There was a commotion at the end of the park, someone shrieked, dogs barked, but sandy-blonde and ball cap just stood still, staring across the street.

Then, as if on signal, they stepped in the same direction. They walked from the court towards the park restroom. Their gait was unusual. Their arms did not move while their legs stepped in rhythm. They disappeared behind a bush for a few moments.

Jacob was upright. His left hand on the wheel while his right held the key in the ignition. Whatever happened, he was ready. He took in a long breath, licked his lips, and blinked three times, but his gaze never wavered from the kids.

The sandy-blonde emerged from the foliage holding a metal pipe walking toward the courthouse. In a moment, he walked past the courthouse and headed towards a long row of well-kept older homes. There was a giant, three-story Victorian that had spiral turrets and a sprawling wooden deck. The house was on the historic register, and people often stopped on Main Street to get a picture. The blonde disappeared along the side of the Victorian.

Ball cap emerged with two smaller pipes. He headed toward the neighborhood, too. There were two other houses, not as grandiose as the Victorian, but still magnificent. When ball cap walked across the street towards the house, it happened. The whole scene unfolded in the middle of the intersection in the heart of the "safest area in town."

As ball cap crossed the midline of Main Street, the bullmastiff bit him on the forearm. Perhaps not even 90 pounds, ball cap tumbled to the cement screaming. A flurry of elbows and paws roiled in the center strip of Main. The basset hound pounced into the melee, violently snarling while his floppy ears spread like the comic wings of a bat. The dogs' owner clung to the leashes as she slid across the concrete on her side. She screamed "stop," and the dogs' names, that I couldn't make out, repeatedly.

The b-ballers ran from the court towards the commotion. Some of them, not sure what to do, circled around the kid with their palms up. One threw a basketball at the bullmastiff while another kicked the basset hound. The traffic in both directions screeched to a halt. A middle-aged man bounded from his pickup. He was screaming *Hey! Hey!* and he kicked one dog in the snout with a booted foot.

A cop emerged from the police station. He absorbed the scene through wide eyes, briefly watching the dogs tearing into the kid. His hand went to his pistol, and his fingers wrapped around the butt of the gun. As he withdrew his weapon, he aimed it at the raging bullmastiff just fifteen feet away. The cop shook his head as if he needed a second to further process the unfolding scene.

I expected him to fire and squinted my eyes in anticipation of the blast.

Somewhere nearby there was a sucking sound. It was so loud it filled the air. "*Ooooommmppp.*" As if a massive set of lungs pulled all the oxygen from the entire neighborhood. The drapes on the old Victorian house flew inward through all the windows on the first floor. There was a silent pause, then a tremendous explosion. Shattered glass and wood splinters flew in every direction. The blast sent everyone on Main backward. I felt the heat even from inside the Buick down the block. A caustic stench of ammonia filled the air. Black smoke poured from the broken windows. In less than thirty seconds, the three-story Victorian was a brilliant monolith of white-hot flame.

The dogs bolted from the explosion. Many of the basketballers struggled to their feet and ran backward. The cop pulled himself up off the street and frantically disappeared into the station. Seconds later, a half-dozen uniformed officers and city employees were out in the road looking at the blaze. Like the videos of the Mount Saint Helens' explosion, the inferno inspired awe. Everyone nearby stood and admired the fire as it consumed the house.

The wind spread to the police station and neighboring houses. The Victorian was a hundred-foot square of dried wood. Mixed with a virulent chemical, it became a veritable inferno.

Inside the Victorian, from within the forest of flames, a man emerged from the front door. He stood in a place of heat so ferocious it seemed impossible. His hair was on fire, and his clothes clung to his body in a jacket of flames. White dripping fell from his arms as he walked across the porch. It took me a minute to realize that this was his skin, falling off in melting sheets. He stumbled on the steps of the porch and tumbled out onto the front lawn, screaming. With all b-ballers and uniformed cops looking on, he fell to his knees in front of a police officer in an agonizing prayer stance. No one helped as he screamed. They stared, captivated by the agony until the man collapsed into a sizzling heap of human flesh.

My hand reflexively covered my mouth. The child attacked by the dogs writhed in the street as the police station just behind him burned. The toxic black smoke from the Victorian caught on a swift breeze and swung toward the burgeoning crowd like a giant snake. Even from inside the Buick, the smell hurt my lungs. Sirens pierced the air as emergency vehicles filled all the empty spots on Main Street. Some of the children were crying as they tended to the bitten child. A beehive of cops, paramedics, and firemen buzzed around.

Amid it all, I saw the sandy-blonde-haired kid walk around the side of the police station. His quaff was matted and burnt. He had soot spots on his face. The metal pipe he held was gone. With a ripped shirt and blood dripping from his neck, he stared into the chaos with a confused look; like he had just woken up in a nightmare and didn't remember falling asleep. He sat down on the curb to collect himself, his chest heaving in panicked breaths.

"What did you do?" I said, looking at Jacob.

But he didn't respond for a long time. He looked out onto the pandemonium unfolding on Main Street with pursed lips and a calm face. Whatever he was thinking, he didn't share.

"Jacob," I said in a whisper, stripping my voice of any emotion. *"What happened to those kids? What the hell is that whistling sound?"*

"I think you should go," he finally said. *"Before* it gets dark." And he looked over at me with earnest eyes. There was nothing extra in those eyes, no exaggeration or attempt to scare. Just the plain fact that Token-Oak was slipping into the abyss.

———————

The national media ran with the story. A spectator took a picture of the kid mauled on Main with the burning police station sign and the Victorian inferno raging in the background. It looked third-world, like something a war correspondent would send back from Chechnya or Tikrit, even though the pic was in the breadbasket of America, not some distant war-torn battleground a world away. The pic ran on the third page of the *New York Times* and had an excerpt on *Sixty Minutes*.

The city of Token-Oak owned the old Victorian. A few city cops and employees were running a meth lab in the basement with air scrubbers and 500-gallon vats. For over a decade, the lab had produced fifty pounds of the high-grade crystal every day. They loaded it up in the trunk of police cruisers and drove it out to distributors. Token-Oak meth went through a network that stretched to hundreds of rural counties. Its tentacles reaching all the way to Washington State and the Everglades. As rival dealers popped up, Token-Oak cops would bust labs within their jurisdiction. They used their influence to organize federal raids and the drug task force to eliminate other dealers.

After ten years of clandestine operation, the newspapers claimed, the lab was discovered when an exterior gas pipe burst and an electrical short-circuit on the breaker panel ignited the blaze. The *Times* called it a "one-in-a-million coincidence," a "freak accident" that exposed the most successful domestic narcotics manufacturer in the Midwest.

After the fire, something "snapped" in Token-Oak. It had been a long time since people called life in Token-Oak bucolic, though the townspeople pretended that it was just a downturn. Life was peaks and valleys, and the last few years in Token-Oak were the nadir. Things would eventually improve, they always had. After the Victorian, however, people gave up the ghost. The media lambasted the residents for not "seeing the blight." Pictures of the fire ran nationally for a solid week. The jokes that followed cut to the bone. Sometimes, all it takes to understand how far a thing has fallen is to listen to the jokes.

I left Token-Oak that morning and didn't look back for a long time. There were images from the trip I carried with me. The Mexican that came into Jacob's store. Those two kids on the basketball court. Most of all, though, I thought about the eyes on the skinhead. When I laid down at night, I saw them—those massive pupils—flashing back. It was like they lived in my memories and lurked in random thoughts. Maybe, I thought, I could leave it all behind. Token-Oak was a tiny town in the middle of nowhere that had no influence on my life. It didn't define me or my future. I'd have to go back when Grandpa and Grandma passed away. But that, I thought, wouldn't be for another decade at least. I borderline prayed that the Smoky Hills around Token-Oak would open and swallow that place into hell.

Sometimes dreams do come true. If you wish for something hard enough, you will it into existence.

The limbs of all those dead branches clawed for me the instant I left.

CHAPTER FOUR:

DEMON TEETH AND BUTTERFLIES

Robert Warrington's Journal
Chicago, Illinois, 1999-2004
5000 days before the Syndemic

After visiting Token-Oak that summer, my personality shifted. I read a lot and spent more time alone. I obsessed over schoolwork and flourished as a student. My junior and senior year of high school, I didn't make a single B. While my friends were out drinking, I worked my ass off to become academically elite. In the winter of my senior year, I submitted college applications to the best programs in the country. I viewed each application as an S.O.S. to passing ships, begging for a chance at a different life, hoping to make it out of the trailer park.

After months of hand-wringing and endlessly checking an empty mailbox, an admittance letter finally came. The University of Chicago admitted me into their undergraduate cognitive psychology program. I left two weeks before classes started. Token-Oak felt far away, like bad music heard from a distance. A thousand miles and millions of people stood between me and the past, but memories still bled through.

College life was full of possibility. Fascinated by the study of the brain, new worlds opened with each class I took. That study was also inspired by Jacob. I wanted to understand what made people like Jacob, the amalgam of genes and environmental influences behind his psychosis. He hung in the back of my mind like a nervous twitch.

I threw myself into behavioral psychology with a frenetic passion. My life was full of schedules, study times, and continuous reading. I approached it all with the rigor of an Olympic athlete. There was this hidden drive within. I hit the books like a doctor inflicted with a terminal illness searching for a cure. There was something so rewarding about studying behavior and the brain like I was trying to solve the riddle of my own shortcomings.

I heard from the grandparents on occasion. Token-Oak was exploding with new people. Most of them were "roughnecks" coming to work on drilling crews or to drive thumper trucks to shoot geological seismic over rolling prairie hills. The meth trade had changed since the fire, but it was spreading at an alarming rate.

Grandpa found telling these Token-Oak stories cathartic, so he laid bare the latest gossip. I consumed these conversations and found myself happy to be five states away. Some of Grandpa's finer analyses included:

> All the fish in Token-Oak's 400-acre Heart Swallow Lake died. The lake was stocked with blue channel cats and crappie. Amid hundreds of the white bellies of dead fish, they found two men and a woman. Their naked corpses were floating face down in the middle of the lake. On the backs of their naked bodies, someone carved a single word: "snitch."

Token-Oak was broke. 85 percent of the children were on assistance. Most school-aged kids had parents on welfare, and the rest received free meals at lunchtime. The local hospital, on average, had four uninsured patients a month that required hundreds of thousands in lifesaving treatment for gunshots wounds and skin grafting for first-degree burns. Each month, there were several meth babies born. The county jail was full, so mandatory releases sent even violent offenders back out onto the streets.

Addicts took over certain areas. Entire neighborhoods in Token-Oak were abandoned. Old Town had rivers of drugs flowing through its alleys. Over half the cinder block homes in Boom Town were cooking drugs, and dozens sat roofless and burned from past fires. There were even a few drug houses in Lakeside. All the while, during the night time, the Hollows and the hilltop were filled with lights of labs working away in the darkness.

There were rampant disappearances. Entire families just up and "moved" out of Token-Oak in the middle of the night. Often abandoning belongings in their homes. The cops were overrun with such reports.

Through it all, Jacob was thriving. Every month he was expanding his sales. He reinvested all his profits into growth. In just under a year, he had stores in five counties and had plans for more in central Nebraska, eastern Colorado, and six in "Methssouri." All right in the heart of meth country.

I had to hand it to him, he was servicing the epidemic like a modern-day Strauss.

My academic career blossomed like a thunderhead over a large body of warm water. I found work with a post-doctorate researcher that was in the middle of a four-year experiment to study novelty pathways in the human brain. His experiment focused on understanding how the brain processed pleasure. The end game was to map the addiction pathway in the brain. It was—as my stoned college roommate often said—completely "next level shit."

As with all human brain research, it began with animal testing. The experiment itself was gruesome. We took laboratory rats and let them "copulate" with rats of different colors. The control group, then the "red group." The red group was simply a cluster of female rats soaked in red dye. The red rats were soaked in red to make them *more attractive* to the males. To study how pleasure affected the brain, we let the rats, as we said in the scientific parlance, copulate. I spent thousands of hours with my hands died beet-red up to the elbow in the belly of the windowless research center watching lab rats fuck.

Immediately after confirming copulation, I guillotined off the rats' heads, peeled the skin off their faces, cracked open the skull with pliers, detached the brain with tweezers from the spinal column, and then froze the brain in a square of gelatin. The killing alone was too much for all but the most intensely serious neuroendocrinology students. The skin peeling, and brain removal was a bridge too far for most.

My post-doc adviser was a Jewish thirty-something, that had crazy hair, named Postitch. He looked like equated intelligence with insane hair and aimed to be the smartest man on earth.

Postitch had a dark sense of humor that took some getting used to. Nonetheless, I worked hard and kept the conversation professional, never reciprocating the playful repartee. Not once did I mention Token-Oak, not once did I reference my past. I never told him I could stomach the slaughter because I grew up in an exceptionally dysfunctional and abusive home on the edge of poverty. I never told him I grew up in a town where you could hear the cries of slaughtered cows on the wind, or you could smell the iron of the blood from the butcher plant when the wind caught you just right. Besides, once you tell people about your past, especially a bad past, you are forever linked with that heritage. I just laughed at his jokes—which were *usually* funny—and pretended to come from an affluent McMansion like all the other kids.

Postitch was obsessed with what he called "the Process." Over years of work, he pioneered a unique style of brain research where he relied on dying microscopically thin slices of freshly removed brains with various dyes. Postitch believed he could study any brain issue using the Process. Over several years, he applied his system to decipher addiction and its connection to the brain stem. No one worked harder than Postitch, as he spent fourteen hours a day crunching the data. He held a tireless work ethic as high as Catholics hold the Pope.

Postitch used various chemicals to discover addiction pathways. Once the brains were frozen, we'd slice them on the microtome—a machine that looked like the most badass meat slicer you ever saw. Then we'd pull the slices onto slides and glue them shut. I spent years of my life looking at cutouts of rat brains.

The rat brain, like a human brain, personifies into abstract evil shapes when sliced just right. I saw frowning faces, demon teeth, and butterflies in those frozen slices. Every slice was unique. All the brains had a story to tell, and Postitch had the ruthless efficiency to translate their stories. I marveled at the complexity of life.

After four years of hard work, our funding ran out. Apparently, our research relied upon federal funding and the grants of two charitable foundations. Postitch warned that money was getting tight and he searched for another source. Some of the other postdocs had studies tied to drug manufacturing and, of course, they never worried about cash. Our research, however, was based on understanding, with a focus on the neural pathways that dealt with the brain stem and lower-level motor functions. In the end, we wanted to reduce, not redesign, prescription medication. Our findings, no matter how groundbreaking, would not "sell."

But Postitch pressed on.

Postitch presented our findings at a behavioral neuroendocrinology conference in Palo Alto, California. I flew out there with him to set up the displays outlining our study. There was a souped-up science fair in a warehouse hangar where "venture capitalists and drug companies" came from all over the world. There was money to be had, Postitch believed, and he searched hard.

We had pictures of the red rats, brain slices, and a map of the brain stem that, we believed, powered addiction-like tendencies. As small groups gathered, Postitch raved about "the Process." How he had pioneered a way to study addiction and the brain through hands-on research and ruthless hard work. Postitch would always end his soapbox speech with the rousing statement, "we believe that we can end addiction." He thought it sounded snazzy as hell. A real drop-the-mic face slapper that was unforgettable.

"Where is the sale?" one particularly erudite doctor said after listening to the speech. "I mean," she said, grabbing Postitch by the shoulder in a friendly manner, "How are you going to fund this thing. You got initial trials, blind tests, and thousands of hours of research on the horizon? Who's going to pay for that? What's the end?" And, it seemed, every single person asked the same variant of those questions. Postitch always said that ending addiction was an end in itself. There was no golden goose, just healthy, happy people. That kind of idealistic talk in a room full of venture capitalists looking to find the next Viagra went over like a fart in a spacesuit.

That night, Postitch and I drank on the cold beaches of Northern California. The waves that crashed were neon, so full of phytoplankton that lines of glowing algae stretched for miles in both directions. The moon was full, and the sky was brilliantly lit with stars. This usually would have Postitch raving for hours about "nature's beauty" or "genetic diversity," two of his favorite subjects. Postitch had a Heineken that he nursed for two hours, just drawing in the wet sand with the end of his bottle. He said very little, which freaked me out. It was hard, I guess, to realize that you spent four years on a project that, according to the group in Palo Alto, was doomed to fail.

When we got back home, he started to box things up in the lab. He had all but thrown in the towel on his research. His family farm back in Israel was on his mind, and I think he was about a week from bolting the United States. He read Henry David Thoreau's *Walden* and started talking about working with his hands. We went on a nature hike together, and it took everything I had to coax him out of the woods back to his Subaru.

It changed with a call from the director of the Animal Research Center about a meeting.

"With a drug company?" Postitch asked hopefully. When the answer came back that it was with a government agency that wanted to "understand our brain stem research," Postitch gave up. "Government, they won't fund shit," he said dismissively. But the director was persistent, and Postitch eventually relented. He agreed to meet with them but promised no enthusiasm.

The next day, Postitch was in the lab when the "government agency" came to visit. An older woman walked in first. Behind her were two guys in suits that shut the door and drew the blinds. They even unplugged the phone line before asking Postitch to take a seat in his own lab. A young man in an ill-fitting suit with a buzz cut directed me to the door.

"I've known him for four years," Postitch said, referring to me. "He's been with me every step of the journey. In many ways, he knows this research better than I do. He ran 90 percent of the tests and extrapolated all the data. Whatever you have to say—if I am the least bit interested, he will be there with me."

The older woman raised her eyebrows at one of the suited men and received a quick nod in response. The two men sat on desks near the door while the older woman spoke.

There was an air of sophistication to the woman, she was older, perhaps fifty. Her eyes had a quiet fierceness that conveyed command. When she spoke, she took a deep breath and stared right into you. Everything she did was well-prepared and carefully examined. The fingers of her hands stood in a sharp steeple in front of her face as she spoke. She introduced herself as Fran Redfearn with an agency that preferred to not be named.

"It's better for everyone that you just focus on the research," she said. "After all, that is what you do. Right?" Fran had studied our findings on addiction and asked—almost like she was laying down a dare—if we were interested in putting our brain stem theory to the test. Fran claimed there were hundreds of subjects that needed to be investigated. She wanted each brain categorized, dissected, stained, and imaged. "The project could take several years to complete. Maybe more. And we need someone that understands the brain stem."

"We need," Fran paused a long time, looking at Postitch, "someone to start next week."

"Well," Postitch said, "I don't have several years. I don't even have a week."

Then Fran did something strange. She leaned in real close and said in a tone that was tantamount to a demand. "We *will* fund your research for another four years. We *will* also wipe out any student debt that you carry. I *guarantee* you admittance as a fellow into the best university in the country. And there *will* be a sizable monthly stipend to allow you to live comfortably during this research." Fran then pointed at me and said, "I'll give him the same deal."

"How much of a stipend?" Postitch said.

"Twenty K."

"I get twenty-eight K every September now," Postitch said with a shrug.

"Let me be clear here," Fran said, scooting towards Postitch, "$20K every month."

A crooked smile spread slowly across Postitch's face as his eyes bounced around the room. He leaned back in his chair. "What's the catch," he finally said.

"You can never discuss the research you do for me with anyone. At any level. For any reason."

The smile slowly slid off Postitch's face.

"Don't you think that will be hard? People come and go out of the lab all the time. It's collegial. Postdocs talk. There are monthly update meetings with the staff. We use our studies to recruit new student researchers. Hell," Postitch said, "how do you think I found this guy." And he hit my knee with the back of his hand. "The open discussion of ideas is part of the scientific process."

Fran leaned in closer to Postitch and said plainly, "Not anymore. You won't do any of the research here. You will move to Cambridge and work in a new lab."

"Massachusetts?"

Fran nodded as her eyes darted from me to Postitch.

"Harvard?" Postitch said. Fran nodded with a sideways grin.

Postitch beamed so brightly that he covered his mouth and looked at the floor. He even squinted his eyes together hard and pulled in a breath. There was a boyishness, an unbridled celebration, occurring inside Postitch he was trying to conceal. At one point, a high-pitched squeal escaped from tightly pursed lips. Postitch stopped for a minute as if he forgot something. He asked in an intense tone, "So... what if... what if, I tell someone? What if it just... *slips out?*"

Fran looked directly into Postitch and held his gaze for a while. "That would be bad."

Postitch frowned and said contemptuously, "How bad?"

Fran frowned back and said nothing. There are people in this world that have "the look." It is a simple stare that requires no physical force, animated gesticulations, or showmanship. It's a genetic trait that rests in the eyes and just behind the forehead. It drops the temperature in rooms by ten degrees and causes Adam's apples to stick in the most masculine of throats. An easy bit of sorcery, "the look" can place second thoughts in a person's mind like a maid leaving a mint on a pillow. Fran had "the look" down to a science. She was almost as fierce as my grandma.

It was as if all the good vibes had been sucked from Postitch. He looked slowly at the two suited men that were sitting on the counters. It was clear now these two were soldiers. And other things went unsaid that floated to the surface. Fran was not the older woman's real name. There was something about the way she said it, it didn't roll out just right. Names are like a pair of well-worn shoes, they take time to mold to you. We also had no idea where these men came from, and the research they wanted was only vaguely explained.

Postitch sensed something now. He puffed his cheeks out as he blew out a breath. He looked at me and asked what I thought. I wagged my eyebrows and tilted my head. We had worked together for a long time, and he understood my meaning.

"So, we take this job, but we can never tell anyone about the research. Correct?"

Fran nodded.

"Well, what will I put on my résumé for the two-plus years I work on this project? You see my concern?"

"I understand," Fran said. "But know this. If you come to work for me, you will be on the front lines of addiction research. You will apply your skills to address the most pressing problem in the country."

Fran scooted her chair even closer to Postitch, and said genuinely, "I watched you at Palo Alto. That is why we are sitting here now. If you really believe you can 'end addiction,' if that goal is more than just an attempt to garner funding, then come work for me. I promise you, after this experience, you will never need another "résumé" again. You won't look for jobs, they will come to you. You will be a millionaire in three years and twice that in six. Money problems will be a distant memory. This opportunity is a game changer regarding career advancement and personal income."

It was a hard sell and a good one. Fran had done her homework on Postitch and pressed the right buttons. She simultaneously appealed to Postitch's desire to change the world while assuaging his fears about future work. The family farm in Israel was hanging in Postitch's mind throughout the conversation, and "Fran" had masterfully pushed it away without insults or threats.

"Alright," Postitch said, "I'll do it if my partner here will do it. There is just one thing, and it's not negotiable."

"What's that?" Fran said.

"I want my money up-front. Two years in advance. No bullshit."

Fran looked at one of the soldiers sitting on the counter. The soldier gave a subtle nod.

"That's fine," Fran said, "then I want you both in Cambridge next Monday. No bullshit."

Postitch reached his hand out. Fran grabbed it and gave it a firm squeeze.

Three hours later, Postitch and I received wire transfers into our respective bank accounts for our two-year stipends. It was more money than I had ever seen in my life. A lifetime of earnings just sitting in an account quietly whispering.

Postitch and I spoke on the phone that night like teenagers. We laughed, cackled really, about the "game changer." We googled the town and imagined ourselves in local bars. Mostly, though, we talked about our past. All the hurdles of life we'd overcome to reach this point. I never mentioned Token-Oak, even then. Though it lurked in my thoughts like a peeping tom.

I should have been thrilled and, outwardly, I guess I was happy. But there was a feeling this money was a payment for more than research services to be rendered. I could go anywhere with this money; the entire world was within my reach now. Financial security, my grandma used to bemoan, is "total freedom."

As I looked at the zeros in my bank account, I was completely motionless. Somehow, I didn't feel free at all.

CHAPTER FIVE:

METH AND HEROIN

Robert Warrington's Journal
Cambridge, Massachusetts 2008-2009
Token-Oak, Winter of 2009
3,000 days before the Syndemic

A week later, Postitch and I watched movers load our belongings into boxes then into a van. We stuffed our clothes and electronics into Postitch's

Subaru and drove I-90 for fifteen hours right through the heart of the Northeast. We stopped in Buffalo, New York, at a roadside diner that looked out on Lake Erie, a frozen slab of ice as far as I could see. Postitch ran the math on a napkin while he sawed into a steak that was as thick as a two by four. He figured in two years, if he stayed frugal, he could save all his money. "I bet they have a cafeteria," he said, waving his fork like a conductor. "I can save on food. And I am banking we can get an apartment near the lab. No gas. No car payment, too." He was elated the rest of the trip. Postitch wanted to retire at forty and was already making plans.

We stopped in Schenectady, New York. Postitch's nerves got the better of him, and he spent a long period in the bathroom at a roadside truck stop. Sure, he was thrilled, but I think—especially looking back now—he knew there would be problems. On the surface, he was ecstatic, but he was in a graffitied stall, on a dirty seat shitting his guts out.

On Monday morning, they had us both in the lab. The set-up was posh. The technology was better than anything we had back in Chicago. It was in a private building well off campus, set apart from any university structures. The entrance was high security: key cards outside, CCTV at every turn, desk guard at the only entrance, retinal scanners, and two vapor locks before reaching the underground facility ten floors below.

After a brief introductory period that consisted of showing us the computers, microtome, and freezer, an assistant brought us our first crate of "samples." It was a massive square of Styrofoam cubes sitting on a wooden pallet. The assistant left Postitch and me alone in the lab. There was not another person on our floor, no students or other postdocs scurrying about. It was quiet except for the sound of an air purification system. The place was nothing but concrete and steel. And sitting there in that basement, listening to the whistling air, looking at the cinder block walls, I felt an eerie pressure, a subtle claustrophobia sweep over me.

Postitch stood and put on some music. He picked an early '60s track named "Run Around Sue." Postitch said music from that era was innocent and still "fresh." Doowop always put him in a good mood, and this was no different. Soon he was dancing around the lab, getting ready to dive into the work.

We unwrapped the first crate and carefully unpacked dry ice layers. The container was huge, probably large enough to house 500 samples at least. We opened it cautiously, giving the wooden slats delicate taps and pulls. Inside the crate, the samples themselves were individually wrapped and packed with more dry ice. When we pulled out the first sample, my jaw nearly hit the floor. I had only dealt with rat brains a little smaller than a ping pong ball. This brain was huge, and there was significant damage to the exterior, a decay that gave it a grey hue.

"What the hell is this," I asked Postitch. "I thought we came here to do *animal* research?"

Postitch looked at me for a long time. I saw all Fran's promises pass through his mind. He was shaken by the sample and unsure how to proceed. Nonetheless, though he didn't know how we would get there, he wasn't willing to throw in the towel.

"We came here to do research," he said.

The frontal lobe was so degraded that it was nearly mush. When Postitch tried to move the brain, portions of it dripped to the floor. If we left it out much longer, we were going to lose the entire sample.

"How do we start?" I said, concerned.

Postitch's eyes narrowed, and he clenched his jaw tight. This was a thousand times the size of anything either of us had seen. It looked impossible, like trying to manipulate a mound of pudding without altering the structure of the pile. But Postitch was determined. He was going to dive into this work.

"We're going to freeze, mold, slice, stain, and then run the numbers. It's no different than what we used to do, just bigger. Now, grab that clipboard and slide it underneath and take it to the deep freeze. Once it's frozen, then we will be able to move it around."

In an hour, we had three dozen brains in the freezer. Then the cataloging started. We worked diligently for an entire day pulling samples and freezing them. Each crate brought a new challenge. Some of the brains were damaged, but most were not. We had all the samples in the first crate frozen by the end of our first shift.

Each of the samples came with a label containing two numbers, two letters, and a surname: "38CMJohnstonM," "48CFSaltrukaO,"

"17BFSingletonM," etc. We taped these labels to the clipboards and started a computer file on each.

"These first numbers — "38," "48," and "17" — are probably ages. The middle stretch, those might be last names," I said.

"Yeah," Postitch agreed, "and the other two letters are race and gender. Caucasian male. Black Female."

I nodded in agreement.

"What is the last letter?" he said.

"Blood type?" I said, guessing.

"Is there an 'M' blood type?" Postitch said, chuckling.

"OK, boy genius, you take a stab at it."

Postitch looked at those letters for a long time and said those letters were a "differentiator," something that categorized the samples into different groups. "It's probably something these brains were exposed to, an environmental or genetic control." He paused for a while, scribbling notes furiously onto a notepad.

Once the first brain was frozen solid, we pulled it from the deep freeze and mounted it on the microtome. As the machine took tiny slices, two things became immediately apparent. The outer fold of the brain was dead tissue. Judging from the cellular decay, it had been lifeless for a while. But the brain stem and the cerebellum were very much alive. In fact, they had actually grown larger and looked more pronounced than in a typical brain.

It was immediately clear why Postitch was chosen to lead this research. The parts of the brain that were the cornerstone of his research—areas long cast aside by his colleagues and the scientific community as only for motor function and coordination—were the only living portions. I could see his eyes spinning. Thoughts and theories crackled through his mind. I don't think he slept for a week.

Certain people lose themselves in their work. Their focus becomes so intense they lose the ability to small talk. Basic functions, such as eating and bathing, become secondary to the work. These people are savants and serial killers or, like Postitch, just damned fine brain researchers.

One night, we were working in the lab past dinner. Postitch wanted to catalog a new batch of samples we'd received. These were a little different than the previous set. In most of the samples, both outer lobes were decayed, and the brain stem, cerebellum, and amygdala were still very pronounced.

Yet these brains, which were all labeled with an "O," had a more vibrant color.

Then we opened a new crate, all samples labeled with an "M," and the ammonia smell was so bad, we had to put on respirators to transfer the new samples to the deep freeze. One of the nameplates caught my eye. It read "24CMMcGuillicuddyM." Back in Token-Oak, the oldest business in town was McGuillicuddy's Mortuary. And I remembered that the proprietor of the building had a son that was about my age. Randal McGuillicuddy, I thought, but could not remember. I chuckled to myself, thinking about that unusual name. I let the thought go and continued my work.

That night, just when we were opening a new crate, Postitch noted the overpowering smell again on boxes labeled with an "M." "Do you smell that?" he said, inhaling deeply through his nose. There was always a repugnant smell when dealing with preserved tissue. The stabilizers used were powerful and filled the room with a capillary-tightening stench. The smell was so pervasive, you'd often catch it again in your hair and clothes. In fact, I learned never to bring food into the lab—especially bread—because it would sponge in the smell. It basted everything in a chemical taste.

"That's formaldehyde," I said, dismissing the question.

"No, it's something else. Something sharp. It burns your nose hairs to breathe."

And I took another pull of the air. Smell is the strongest sense tied to memory. The right concoction can take you back to a moment, an olfactory version of time travel. At that moment, standing there in the belly of the epidemiology lab behind two vapor locks, I remembered Token-Oak. That twitch junky stealing anhydrous ammonia from my grandfather's truck when I was just a boy. The way his rotten teeth seethed as he breathed watching Jacob and me. It was like you could see the addiction running inside him like that creature from *Aliens* just wanting to break out of his chest. That smell brought it all flooding back, right down to the boyish wonderment that I felt standing there on Grandma's driveway.

"That's ammonia," I said to Postitch. "I'd put my life on it."

He gave me three sharp nods while he pursed his lips just staring at the brain.

"That's it. This brain is saturated in ammonia," he said. Postitch looked around the sample from every angle. The brain had a grey decay on top, though underneath, the brain stem and the systems surrounding it were thriving.

"Look at this," Postitch said as he held up one of the samples so I could see underneath. "Most of the higher-level functioning has disappeared. But the motor and balance of this person would have been incredible. Let me show you something," Postitch said as he loaded slides he had made of previous samples into a microscope.

He loaded a half dozen slides until he found what he wanted. Then he loaded the slide onto a computer screen and pointed to two almond-shaped regions on both the left and right side. Each was very pronounced and reddish in color. "Those two spots are the amygdala. The fear... the fight-or-flight regions. It's our baser brain. And they are very much alive in all these subjects."

He looked at each slide for several minutes, explaining the subtle differences in each sample while outlining the similarities. To Postitch, each brain was a new amazement. He never tired and he grew more excited as he slid new slides into place. "Every human," he said, staring up at the projected microscopic image, "is infinitely complex." He could have stared out those slides forever, a trait I always admired and found annoying before lunchtime.

"Before these people died, what do you think they were like?" I said. We had never talked about where the sample came from or the people they used to be. I assumed it was best to avoid the discussion. The research was hard enough without humanizing the samples.

Postitch shook his head while looking at a brain scan. He had this habit of blinking several times before he delivered an opinion that was sure to ignite a debate. "I think," he said with two fingers covering his mouth, "they would have been incredible. People with exceptional motor control that were driven by fear and aggression. Without a properly functioning cerebrum, they may have been very dangerous. Both to themselves and anyone nearby."

But he shook off the thought and said it was impossible to live in that state. That these brains were likely removed and then soaked in a chemical within minutes of removal. It was the only way that outside lobes of the brain were rotting while the interior—the brain stem, cerebellum, and the amygdala—were thriving.

"There is one thing that I do not understand," Postitch said, looking at the decayed fissures and rotten hemisphere of a brain sitting on the table before us. He paused for a long time, perhaps an entire minute before saying, "it doesn't make any sense." He paused again for another minute.

"What?" I said finally. Postitch took a deep breath then started to speak. He stopped himself and then he began again. Stammering a second time he smacked his hand on the stainless-steel table. Whatever he was trying to say, wasn't coming out easily.

"The brain stem is still alive."

"Right," I said, "surrounded by dead tissue. I get it."

"No," he said with a touch of anger, "it's still alive after we freeze it."

"That's impossible," I said. "The cell walls would have broken from freezing.

He stopped looking at the brain for a minute and focused his attention on one of the CCTV cameras in the corner. Then he looked back at me and said in a whisper. *"The brain stem in the samples is still intact."*

Two weeks after we started, Fran arrived at the lab. Late in the afternoon, she walked in with a rectangular attaché and three uniformed soldiers. There was a curious energy in the room. It wasn't frantic, not exactly, but all business. Fran went right to the conference table without speaking and spread out documents. She sent one soldier to track down a coffee and had another set up a high-definition projector. The third, clearly an officer, sat across from Fran at the conference table. Postitch and I were working in the back when she called us for a meeting.

"Alright, gentlemen, show me why I paid you," she said, looking at Postitch through wire-framed glasses. "Did you have trouble adjusting to the lab?"

"We were expecting rat brains," Postitch said. "It was a surprise, but we've done fine."

"Good," Fran said, "I knew you would. I see you've processed all the crates." Postitch nodded. Fran then asked him to outline his findings

Postitch broke down each crate we'd received into demographic groups. He analyzed them by the label. A projector displayed brain cross sections, and Postitch set the display to run a cascade of slides that each appeared for a millisecond. The effect was a 3D flash of each brain. Postitch spoke at length about the outer decay of the brains and the thriving brain stem, cerebellum, and amygdala in each sample. He used a laser pointer to highlight specific sections. I'd never seen him more prepared or organized. After an hour and fifteen minutes, he asked for comments

"*Excellent*," Fran said, taking off her glasses and setting them down on the conference table. She proceeded to lay out directives on how to further process the data. More shipments were coming, she explained, on a regular schedule for the foreseeable future. Fran paused for a moment and placed her palms on the table. She sniffed the air around him and looked around the lab. "What is that," she said, squinting her eyes.

"Yeah," Postitch said, "can you tell the person preserving the samples to ease up on ammonia, OK? The smell—it's powerful—soaks into my clothes. On some crates, we have to wear respirators when we open them."

"The ammonia?" Fran said.

"Whatever they're soaking these in when they're removed. Can you please tell them to reduce the soak? It's particularly bad on samples that end with M."

Fran looked at the officer across the table. It was a half second glance, but something exchanged between them. I felt the thought floating through the air. And the feeling was that of quiet tension. Fran then glanced back at Postitch and said, "have you documented the difference in smell between each crate?"

"I document everything. We've got a data point for the smell."

"Good," Fran said, "anything else?"

"One more thing," Postitch said as he pulled up another slide. He aimed his laser pointer at the screen and circled it around an area of live tissue surrounded by an area of grey brain decay. "This area here," he said, "this is still alive." Postitch zoomed in to the cellular level. On the screen, there was a series of cell walls still intact. Postitch explained that the part of the brain was still living, even after the deep freeze. "This portion of the brain is resilient to extreme stressors."

Postitch stopped for a moment. He allowed Fran to interject an opinion. But she stayed silent. Assuming that he was not clear, Postitch rephrased and continued, "I mean this is living tissue. That brain stem tissue is completely preserved."

Postitch paused and looked at Fran. He waited for an explanation. When none came, he waded in further.

"So . . ." Postitch continued, "what do you soak these in before they come to me? Can you find out how they preserve these samples? Whatever it is has an incredible effect on the brain."

Fran looked at the officer across from her. Another thought past between the two. This time both looked at Postitch. The officer folded his arms and Fran said nothing.

"It would benefit the research if we had all the information," Postitch said softly.

"Postitch," Fran said, setting her glass on the table, "I brought you here for one reason. You are to process these samples and report on them in the format provided. You've done that. These questions are not relevant to the project."

"Not relevant?" Postitch said. He shook his head. Postitch had spent the better part of his life turning over minute details to uncover new data sets. The smallest minutia could change an experiment. Overlooked and ignored statistics often made the difference between ground-breaking discovery and abject failure. Postitch had the heart of a great researcher and endlessly cataloged everything. He was unaccustomed to walls to information. Frustrated, he reached for something that was likely too far.

"Where do you get these samples?" Postitch said with a hint of defiance.

"How's that?" Fran said.

"I was just wondering, where you get these brains. There are so many. Some of them are young. And yet they just keep coming every week by the hundreds. So... *where do they come from?*"

Fran started to speak, but the officer raised his hand. The officer turned his chair to face Postitch. He was a stout man in his fifties that had no hair and liver-spotted skin. The officer had a gruff voice that was low and matter-of-fact. "You focus on the work we give you. You do good work. At the end of your contract, you may leave with no issues." The officer then paused for a long time and looked at Postitch with a borderline glare.

Fran thanked us. She asked if there was anything we needed to improve the research. Postitch asked for a few software programs and a chromatograph. A minute later, the meeting was over. Fran, the officer, and the soldiers were headed topside.

After they left, Postitch was genuinely troubled. "Did you hear what that son-of-a-bitch inferred? We can leave with no issues at the end of the contract *if* we do a good job." Postitch clenched his jaw and looked at the corner of the room.

"Sure, I'll do the work, but I will find out what is happening here. You can bet your life on that."

Besides the tension with the officer, life settled into a comfortable rhythm. I continued my education at one of the best schools in the world. Even though the admission rate was in single digits, I didn't even apply. Postitch and I found loft space above a bustling arts district. From my bedroom window, I saw the steeple of a Catholic church built in the eighteenth century. The gentle ringing of bells filled my ears throughout the day. I'd found peace and, it seemed, put as much distance between myself and Token-Oak as possible. Deep down, I felt removed, like that small town was no longer part of me.

For the next year, more samples came. We continued to process them and refine the data. I completed my master's degree and started working toward my doctorate.

Late one night in October, I received a call from Token-Oak. My phone rang and, as I felt it vibrate in my pocket, I could tell it was reaching for me. My stomach turned, and I felt eyes on the back. Deep in the belly of that brick building, I heard the rustling of trees. The not-so-subtle shaking of dead branches clicking together in high winds.

"Bob." It was Grandpa, and there was pain in his voice. He told me Grandma had had an aneurysm and I needed to come home. He said, in his general way of putting things, that I needed to hurry "the fuck up."

I hastily packed and called Postitch. He promised to handle things in my absence. An hour later, I hit the highway and barreled toward the center of the country. Somewhere on the interstate while on the outskirts of a town called Hannibal, I got another call.

"She's gone, Bob."

"What?"

"She was dead long before she got to the hospital. The doctors called it a 'brain bleed.' And she died right there on the kitchen floor."

I told Grandpa "sorry" and then listened into the phone. There was a long, awkward silence. And I wondered if he was crying. The old German never displayed genuine sadness. Of course, he was prone to fits of rage, but depression was not part of his palette of emotions. I waited for him to speak as I listened to the sound of rubber tires echo off the highway. I pushed my ear into my iPhone, hoping the pressure itself would elicit a reply.

"You still coming?" he finally said.

"Yeah, I'm coming. Be there in a few hours." Once I left the interstate, I drove like a fiend through unlit, two-lane country roads that twisting over and through fields of dead crop stubble and barbed wire fences. The hood of my car swallowed the night air as it rolled towards Token-Oak.

My thoughts drifted to Grandma, when you lose somebody that was such a big part of your life there's this gaping hole the person occupied. There is love and yearning to see them again, but there's so much more. Emotional moments you shared together—especially the hard times and struggles—crowd over you like a thick blanket. Naturally, I thought about that chilly afternoon on Grandma's driveway playing basketball with Jacob. I thought about how she had slapped me to the linoleum floor of the kitchen. Probably in the same spot where she died. I thought about the way—when she was *furious*—she seemed to vibrate and, more than anything, I thought about her warning. "Bob," she had said decades earlier, you're gonna need him "for what's coming." Maybe she was right, perhaps she was wrong. Now she was dead, and I never would be able to talk to her again.

I arrived at Grandma's house just past midnight. I pulled up, and the basketball goal was still hanging over the detached garage at the end of the driveway. I stopped at the crack we always considered the free throw line and looked up at the hoop. The wind was whistling through the trees and twisting around buildings. The constant shift in the gusts produced a howling sound. And the net on the goal—probably the same net we used as kids—hung on a single strand, flailing like a child's tantrum.

As I stood there, watching it twist in the wind, the last strand tore, and the net dropped to the concrete driveway below. It had hung there for two decades. Endured a thousand storms. Yet it tore as I stood there and watched. The chances of such a thing were infinitesimal. A lightning strike or lotto type of odds. That was Token-Oak. It was the town's way of saying "welcome home." Welcome back to a place where long odds and devilish occurrences are commonplace.

I looked up at the kitchen window as I had done as a kid, and I realized then I expected to see Grandma. It was the first time that I started to cry since I heard the news.

I walked up the stairs leading to the kitchen. The same old linoleum floor was still there. The spot near the stove, the very place where I lay as a kid, was directly in front of me. I looked over and saw Grandpa sitting at the kitchen table quietly reading the newspaper. He had a concerned look on his face like he was focusing on the words and he didn't bother to say hello. Ever since I was a little kid, he had these brooding moods where he didn't want to talk. Not only that, he didn't want to hear any talking either. He would just sit, scowl, breathe heavy and let out low grunts. I learned long ago to let him simmer. Sure, his wife had died, his life was forever changed, and I hadn't seen him in person in over three years. But rules were rules, and I let him be.

I pulled up a chair and grabbed the nearest magazine. I sat there for five minutes in silence reading the sports section about the local girls' basketball teams. Finally, Grandpa slid the spectacles off his face and set them on the table. Rubbing his eyes with his index fingers, he said, "I need to go to Zion Lutheran. So..." he then let out an exasperated breath, and said, "Let's go."

"It's 1:00 a.m. in the morning," I said.

"The pastor lives there. It's always open. Besides, I tithed the last fifty years every Sunday."

A few minutes later, we drove over to the church. Grandpa wanted to speak to the pastor about the funeral service. We walked right into the chapel. I sat in a room full of stained-glass windows looking up at a life-sized wooden carving of Christ that hung over the altar. Gramps disappeared through a side door for a half hour. Though I never saw the man, I know Gramps woke the pastor and harangued him about some minutia surrounding the service. I envisioned a sleep-drunk octogenarian trying to be polite while Gramps demanded macaroons in the foyer and *"What a Friend We Have in Jesus"* on the organ.

After Church, we made a trip across town to McGuillicuddy's Mortuary. It was just past 2:00 a.m. but Gramps said Mr. McGuillicuddy also "lived on site," like that fact encouraged late night visits. I sat in the lobby of the funeral home, a mom-and-pop establishment that claimed to be the oldest business in Token-Oak. The sign said it first opened during the Civil War. Pictures adorned the walls with corpses in pine boxes with silver dollars in their eyes. The dead used to sit outside like a bag of mulch at a hardware store. The place clung to its 1860 roots with spittoons in each corner of the lobby and the famous horse-drawn hearse that was part of the business's logo.

Grandpa was gone for quite a while, but he reappeared with a single question:

"Do you want to see her?" he said in a voice far too cheery for the surroundings.

"See who?"

"Now, who the hell do you think," Grandpa said. I should have objected, or flatly said "no." But I stood and started walking with Grandpa down a long hallway that descended gradually lower. The hall wrapped around the building itself with three turns until it reached the basement annex. We arrived at the end of a rectangular room.

There were coffins lined up like cars in a garage. One of them, at the very end of a row, was open under a single spotlight. A suited funeral director stood before it and waved at Gramps like he was guiding a 747 on the tarmac with an illuminated wand.

The lid on this coffin was open and washed in orange light. Grandpa and I shuffled in on one side to look at Grandma. With an obsequious bow, the funeral director slipped away with his arms tucked behind his back. He was lurking in the corner nearby while purposefully keeping his distance. No doubt a necessary skill learned when dealing with grieving families.

I was afraid to look at Grandma, so I kept my eyes on my shoes. Grandpa shifted in his stance and let out a single questioning grunt: "hmmmmm?" The type of sound someone emits when they are questioning something.

"It can't be," he finally said. I closed my eyes and reached up to pat him on the back.

"No, it cannot be. It just can't." I rubbed his back harder and with more force. I thought he was struggling to accept the grief, still in the throes of denial of his wife's passing. Gramps said in an unmistakably angry tone. "Who the fuck is this, Mac?"

The funeral director looked up from the floor at Grandpa. He walked around the corner and peered into the coffin.

"That is not my wife, Mac, goddamnit! And if it is, you did the worst fucking job I have ever seen in my life. You, goofy ass sumbitch. I always knew hanging out with corpses made a man weird, but I guess it makes him dumb, too? You, split-coat-tail, top-hat-wearing fucking idiot!" And the remainder of Grandpa's rant was a tapestry of profane insults woven together in a dexterous rage.

The funeral director apologized *profusely*. He had opened the wrong coffin. The person we were looking at had a head wound that was not entirely covered. The funeral director tried to politely guide Gramps from the basement so he could switch the coffins. Grandpa slapped at Mr. McGuillicuddy's hands and pointed in his face threatening to "stamp a ticket to federal *goddamn* prison" if he touched him again. Gramps kept yelling *"find my wife,"* with a mouth open so wide I could have set a can of soda between his teeth. Grandpa's screams echoed off the brick walls of the basement so intensely, I felt the reverberation pressing down upon me. "Find my wife... Find My Wife... FIND MY WIFE!"

Grandpa took to flipping open coffin lids in a rage. The first, thankfully, was empty. The second had Grandma, and the sight of her bought him to a dead stop, the way the bright lights of TV suddenly occupies a tantrum-throwing toddler. The snarl on his face slid away and both his hands clutched the side of the coffin with a gentleness that seemed impossible. I moved in toward his left to see.

Grandma had a pastel-colored face. For whatever reason, the Undertaker tried to manipulate her expression into a subtle smile, but it wasn't a good look. Grandma looked like she was holding a devilish secret. I couldn't look at her.

I hated the American death ritual. The way that we "honor" our dead is downright macabre. To take the person that meant so much to us, fill them full of chemicals, stretch their face into a rubber mask, then manipulate their skin into a permanent expression that epitomized their personality. Taxidermized animals had it better. At least all their friends didn't have to see them slightly smiling. The very core of this ritual is disgusting *at best*.

"She looks beautiful," Grandpa said.

"Yeah," I said in response, not wanting to offend.

"There is something I never told you, Bob. About the time she died. It's best I tell you here."

I looked down at the floor and frowned. Tact was never something I associated with my grandfather. To him, apropos was an island in the Caribbean where affluent New Yorkers got drunk and raced yachts. This was far from the best time. In fact, there may not have been a worse time to hear such talk. But Grandpa waded in chest deep. He continued:

"When I walked in and saw her on the floor, she wasn't dead. I hit the top of the stairs and reached down to check her. Before I could do anything, she grabbed me and pulled me down to her face. She only glared—the way she used to—and she shot me *that look*. You remember the look? How she'd shake in anger?"

"I remember."

"It was like she was warning me. She wanted me to know something but couldn't say it. I saw it in her eyes."

There was a long silence then. Standing next to his wife in the basement of the mortuary, I saw Grandpa shaking his head and biting his bottom lip. After a while, he said, "this is it. The last time you'll be alone with her. Say what you need to." And he stepped away.

I switched places with him so I could be near the head of the coffin. I leaned down real close to Grandma's face. My mouth was near her ear. There were things that I wanted to say, even things that I had to say, but nothing came out. My mind locked up like a bad transmission. And I stood there with the tips of my fingers wrapped around the cold titanium of the coffin, thinking about all my inadequacies. A better grandson would have said something sentimental and touched her hand gently. But I was not that person. Not that day, at least.

Grandpa and I didn't speak again until we got into the car. We drove through Token-Oak in the middle of the night in silence. It was past 3:00 a.m. and a cold chill had settled around the town. We drove down Main Street, past all the small-town staples: the Elks club, the Eagles, and the VFW. They were all excuses where red-nosed, whiskey drunks could get plastered without having to lose face by going to a honky-tonk. But even these places were closed.

As we turned onto Grandpa's street, there was a group of three people walking along the sidewalk. Another person was behind them carrying a baseball bat along one of his legs like he was trying to conceal it and not doing a very good job. They were dressed in all black and hard to spot in the darkness. Just as I started to notice them, one slipped over a fence, another disappeared behind a house, and the third melded into the night.

"Shit," Grandpa said as he watched the three figures. "They're everywhere now."

"Who," I said.

"I dunno. But they've always been in this town. Even when I was a kid. There was a half a hundred living in the hollows way back in the '50s. But they kept their distance then. Their kids never went to school, and they didn't even come into town to buy groceries. They were just "fat of the land" drifters. Some believed they were a commune of motorheads. Maybe some post-war communists that didn't want to be fucked with."

We pulled into Grandpa's driveway and put the car into park. Grandpa swung his neck to look out the windows of the vehicle. He was checking all the dark spots around the garage and underneath the trees.

"But now, they're everywhere. Crawling through town at night. Thieving. I swear there must be a thousand."

"Come on now," I said, smirking. But I didn't leave the car and started looking around.

"You come on. Paul Millsap crop dusts and flies that Cessna Ag-wagon—the little fixed-wing. You know Paul? He wears the goggles offset on his head and drinks those yellow drinks all over town.

"Frozen margaritas?" I said.

"Hell, yes. Has 'em at the bank while standing in line, in the drive-through at the Tasty Freeze. Hell, I even saw him with one while he was shoveling snow off his driveway. Anyways… Paul buzzed over the Hollows a few times in the past year. He swears there are shanties every acre underneath those thickets of dead oaks. There are thousands of people out there. And more of them come in off the highway every day."

"Come on, Gramps. Don't you think that people would notice?"

But he just shook his head slowly while making eye contact. He let out a long sigh and pulled his thin hair back across his head. Once so proud and thick, Gramp's hair had disintegrated into long, white strands. With his liver-spotted scalp exposed and his gaunt frame, Gramps—for the first time in his life—looked haggard.

We walked inside and sat in the cool of the basement. I could tell he wanted to talk. He kept pacing around adjusting things. As with all things with Grandpa, I had to let him arrive at his own time.

Eventually, he told me Jacob hadn't been home in a year. He'd left long before Grandma had a stroke. And, Grandma believed that he was living in the Hollows. And, according to Grandpa, that fact alone, "stressed Grandma so bad she had a stroke and died." It didn't matter that Grandma smoked a pack of cigarettes a day for fifty straight years, had a genetic history of stroke, and never exercised. To Grandpa, Jacob's behavior killed Grandma, *"end of story."*

For the first time in his life, Grandpa talked about the dark side of Token-Oak. I'd heard him mumble a few things in the past about the town. How the dying oaks were a "sign from God," or how the Hollows was where "the dead could talk." But he never elaborated on any of these statements. It's like he didn't want to know these things. Speaking about them just breathed life into the very thing he was willfully ignoring. Our family never talked about the Hollows. Losing a family member changes a person. It causes a revaluation and new approach. It just so happened I was there for the transition.

Grandpa laid bare his thoughts about Jacob and decades of repressed feelings came pouring out. "He'd become one of those thieving fuckers. Every time I saw them at night dressed in their black clothes, I'd wonder if it was him. They're growing, Bob. And it's not like it used to be. They're every goddamn place now."

Gramps told me about the people that were controlling the Hilltop. How they all had the same physical characteristics—which was odd because they were different sizes. They generally wore dark clothes and had deep-socketed eyes and loose skin. There was this grease that hung about them, the kind of sweat layer that comes from little sleep and poor hygiene. Whenever they entered a Token-Oak restaurant or grocery store, a quiet hush fell over the entire building. Each of them had a presence that was downright commanding. All types of people were involved in this group. They were black, white, old, young, rich, and poor. They generally lived out around the Hilltop in mobile homes and RVs. Though some stayed in lean-tos and handmade shanties like Paul Millsap had seen. Grandpa believed there were thousands of them and claimed they ruled the nighttime like feudal lords. He argued that the way people around the county catered to them was astounding: local police, county commissioners, and even a few on the highway patrol.

There were different nicknames for the denizens of the Hollows. The cops called them transients because they were always moving around to different sides of the Hollows. Local farmers and people living outside of town called them merely "the thieves." It seemed like anything that wasn't bolted down in the country just disappeared. Copper wire, tools, generators, car stereos, used tires, and even family pets were favorite targets of the thieves.

The pastor at Zion Lutheran that talked about the Hollows like it was hell on earth. His sermons were doom and gloom and filled with warnings. The Bible, to him, was little more than a warning label. He spared no one, not even the angels. Those winged deities could sin just like anyone else. He continually repeated a verse that said God did not spare angels when they sinned, instead he committed them to the chains of gloomy darkness to be kept until judgment. The fallen angels of Token-Oak came—at least most of the time—from good homes and families that loved them. Only to walk the Hilltop and lose themselves. There was one immutable truth about the "Fallen" that not once was ever proven wrong: once a person walked into the Hollows, they never came back. Not the same, at least. Not once. And everybody in town knew it. That was why parents pulled their kids close when the Fallen walked into a Token-Oak store. That is why people, including Grandpa, only whispered secrets about the Hollows. Because they didn't want to get involved. The Hollows was Token-Oak's darkest secret that everyone could see when they looked northeast of town.

"I knew what was up there," Grandpa said. "Kids talked about that place, but nobody went. It was like you could feel the evil. When I was a kid, traveling gypsies came through town during the County Fair. They made money doing palmistry and tarot readings. They did psychic readings where everyone sat in a circle and called the dead. What do they call those things?"

"A séance," I said.

"Right. Well, they made a big show of it. Charged per head and piled people into a tent. And started reading the room. They had this clairvoyant lady with a bandana and long fingernails take questions about dead loved ones from the crowd. She'd pause at each inquiry, breathe it in while her eyes fluttered, and then 'speak' from the beyond. It was smoke and mirrors. If I had to describe it in a word, it would be kitsch. Most of it was a joke, and it was meant to be. 'Tell me about my grandma,' someone would yell. Her eyes would flutter, and she'd say, 'you still can't cook, and you haven't read the bible in two decades.' People would hoot and howl, and she'd move on.

"But there was one lady, I can't remember her name. Her son returned from the Korean War and walked into the Hollows. They found his body in the same ditch where they always dumped the dogs. He was stripped bare, and his fingers were cut off. Well, this woman stood up in the tent and asked the clairvoyant, 'how is my son... is he still in the Hollows.' I swear you coulda heard a mouse fart in that tent. The clairvoyant did her thing. The deep breath, the eye flutter. She raised one hand to her mouth and the other out to the crowd. Then she just paused. And I mean it was for a full minute. She just stood in the tent surrounded by candles and people from Token-Oak looking on.

"A wind cut through the tent flaps. The candles they had lining the edges of the tent flickered, and some went out. Then the clairvoyant's nose started to bleed. A little trickle at first, then a full pour. Her eyes shot open, and she coughed, spraying blood onto the front row. She stumbled backward as she screamed. Most of it was nonsense, but there was one thing she kept saying over and over, "Dämonen Zucht! Dämonen Zucht! Dämonen Zucht!"'"

"What does it mean?" I asked.

"It's old-style German. It means 'demons breeding.'

"*Jesus*," I said.

Grandpa nodded and continued, "Those gyppos grabbed that clairvoyant and drug her to the back of the tent. She started frothing at the mouth and screamed in English, '*they'll come from those hills and kill you all.*' It was the damnedest thing I ever saw. The gyppos closed the tent that night and started packing up. In the morning, that clairvoyant wasn't in her trailer. Someone pulled her right through the window, right off her bed."

"What happened after that?"

"Nothing. There was a police report filed, but they never found her. The gypsies never came back to Token-Oak," Grandpa said as he poured himself another drink.

Grandpa looked around the basement then. He was holding a highball of Wild Turkey and took a pull. There was a window not much larger than a two-foot rectangle along the basement wall near the ceiling. He stared into the blackness of that hole for a good minute.

"No one in this town talks about it because it listens. This goddamn town listens. You talk too much about it, and you'll disappear, too. Everyone knows the drill."

Grandpa looked at the black window then and sneered and said, "But you reach a point," he continued in a hushed tone, *"where fear can't control you anymore.* My wife is..." he gripped his whiskey and nodded, closing his eyes. "And now those fuckers have my grandson... you reach a point where you are not afraid to die. It's just a matter of time before they come for me."

"Gramps," I said, not wanting him to get too worked up.

"No. They will come. Your grandma always said they would. I thought she was fucking crazy. We all did. But it was right there staring us in the face the whole time."

There was a pregnant pause. Grandpa had wild eyes that flashed with anger and fear. Then he told me something I don't think he ever shared with another human being.

"They kill families, Bob. All the way down the line. They just pull out the entire tree, stem, branches, and all until the whole thing is dead. I've seen it three dozen times. Some poor kid goes to the Hollows. He's gone a year, maybe more. Then he returns for a day or two. In the week that follows, the kid ends up dead. And the whole family 'moves away.' It wasn't until right now... maybe at this very moment... I realized they never moved away. Those sons of bitches have been murdering people for decades."

He took a long pull of his whiskey, draining the highball. He set the glass on the wooden coffee table with a clank.

"Jacob will come back. Then they'll kill him. Then they'll kill me." Gramps looked at me square in the face. "I imagine they'll eventually come for you, too, if you keep coming around. It makes you wonder just what they are hiding up there."

Grandpa stretched out on the divan and closed his eyes. "I'm done talking about it. I've said all I'm going to say. Now leave me alone, would ya?"

I nodded and stood. "But... just sit with me for a few minutes," he said. "Just sit with me for a few minutes in the dark."

Grandma's wake was that night at McGuillicuddy's Mortuary by Heart Swallow Lake. There were only a hundred chairs in a room with blue carpet, and wood-paneled walls called the "chapel." It looked like a conference room at a cheap motel with dirty carpet, coffee urns stained black with age, and water spots on the suspended ceiling tiles. On the wall, two large tapestries of the Last Supper somehow reminded me of the dogs playing poker picture that adorned every man cave in the Midwest. At the front of the room, there was a rostrum with a microphone.

All the folding chairs were taken in the first few minutes. Token-Oak townspeople were enamored with death. It was rare a funeral wasn't well attended. They always said that they came to pay their "last respects" to "honor the dead" or "comfort the bereaved." Even as a young boy, I understood that was horseshit. They came to see the body and watch the family cry. They wanted to stand close to a corpse and feel the sting of death. After all, it happens to everyone. It's something that few people address until it's too damn late.

There was a line for Grandma's coffin two-deep stretching out the chapel and wrapping around the foyer of the mortuary. Grandpa, always the politician, stood at the rostrum and gave an impromptu eulogy, even though the proper place for such a speech would be at the funeral service at the church. Gramps was a German Lutheran raised on fire and brimstone pulpit pounders who pointed at the audience and shouted their message. After ten minutes, of "she will pound on the pearly gates and demand entry... and JESUS HIMSELF will swing them open!" and "her life was a sonnet that will echo through eternity, and you can COVER YOUR EARS and still hear the music." I couldn't take it anymore. To eulogize Grandma in such a way, at least to me, was ill-placed and borderline offensive. I walked out the front door just to get some air.

"Bha-*aab*," a voice said from the shadows behind. I turned around and saw Jacob sitting in a gazebo with wooden benches surrounding a plastic angel. He took a long pull of a cigarette, sucking the skin to his teeth. Through a deep inhale, he laughed at me with a low body shake then blew the smoke out through his nose. He gave me a nod, acknowledging my presence, and motioned for me to come over and sit.

As I approached, I could see the change on Jacob's face. He had a perpetual thousand-mile stare—something he wanted desperately to have as a child, though he could never achieve it due to youth. Chiseled into his face were deep-set eyes with dark circles. He had wrinkled clothes and unkempt hair like he slept in his car. All the mannerisms he had when he was a kid were still there: the slight tilt of the head and inability to make eye contact, exaggerated emotions, and the entitlement he wore like a coat. As I sat near him, I could feel the tiredness radiate off him like hot air from a space heater. He looked as if the world had been taking little pieces of him each day for a long while.

Dozens of questions swirled in the depths of my mind. Each of them struggled to surface for a gasp of breath. What was he doing at the Hollows? Why had he disappeared? How was he living? Was it possible, were the stories all true... could he talk to the dead? And I was thinking about what to ask when Jacob, as he always did, launched into a dominating monologue.

"Do you remember the *pigs*?" Jacob said. The pupils of his eyes swimming in the deep circles around his sockets. Circles and circles and circles. Like rings of an old oak tree after it was cut down. There was this strangeness that, even now, I can hardly articulate. He took these long, slow breaths. Everything seemed so deliberate. That was an entirely new creation from Jacob.

"I think about that day sometimes," he said. "How we were playing and—BOOM—I woke up to the fire and Grandpa beating me. I have no memory of those pigs. All I know is what the shrinks told me over the years."

"I remember everything about that day," I said.

"You should come up there," Jacob said. He took another long draw on his cigarette, again sucking his teeth down his throat.

"Where?" I said. Even though I knew exactly where he was talking about.

"You'd be amazed. I struggled my whole life to be free. I just wish you could swim in my head; you could understand. You go up there, sit in the circle of rocks... Close your eyes... Shit." He looked over at me and blew out a puff of smoke from deep within his lungs that was so thick it made me cough.

"You're scared," he said, chuckling. "You should be. It's scary shit." He smiled nervously.

For the next minute, Jacob told me about his new businesses. The meth facilitating was still strong, spreading to tiny towns across the Midwest. But there was a new player in nearby midsized towns. A prescription drug—OxyContin—that "everyone" was getting from the new pain clinic in town. For those that didn't have scripts, there was a vibrant network of daily runners selling tiny balloons of pure black tar from a little Mexican town spelled with an X. These runners were all over the nation. They just popped up in the Midwest in Wichita, Oklahoma City, Lincoln, Jeff City, and Des Moines. "It's taking over. In a year, a third of the country will be hooked on something."

"Heroin?" I said. Jacob nodded tightly.

He explained that the advent of "oxy" had changed the drug trade in Token-Oak. Everyone, according to Jacob, knew someone who was hooked. He had clients living in the best houses in town buying $500 of pills a day. Some of it was personal delivery, too. Like Dominos or Chinese takeout. Housewives would walk out of their mansions and across their brick driveways to meet a driver with a handful of pills. The trade had become so common, that the neighborhood of houses on the west side of town was known as the Pill Mansions. Sprawling lawns, personalized wrought iron gates, pool houses, and, apparently, a thriving population of dope fiends.

The rest of the addicts in Token-Oak got their supply of "oxy" the legal way. They filled bottles at the pharmacy written from the new Pain Clinic. You could sit at the west end of Token-Oak and watch the traffic into the Pain Clinic roil and fester like a prairie storm. There was a line stretching around the building from sun up to sun down. At the Pain Clinic, it was black Friday every single day. Some locals stood in a long line outside the building early in the morning only to sell their spot for a few hundred bucks. Word was that prescriptions were so easy to come by, that people drove from over 300 miles away to get a bottle of sixty OxyContin filled. The Pain Clinic had written, according to Jacob, twenty thousand scripts in just over a year. Token-Oak was awash in *legal* narcotics.

"You think I'm trash. Always did." Jacob held his hand and pointed at the open door to the wake. "You think that's the end. You don't know shit." He laughed again, this time standing up.

"Jacob, wait a second… just wait."

But Jacob didn't respond. He lit another cigarette with the one he was smoking. He grabbed the drawstrings of his hood and pulled it taught around his face. Right before he turned to leave, he shot me a look. I'd been on the other side of half a million Jacob looks before, all of them stolen where stolen from a television screen only months prior, but this one was different. Our eyes connected and, as I looked into those dark circles, I saw something new. There was sadness there, a deep yearning. Without speaking, I swear he was crying. In those eyes, I saw an apology flash, then it was gone.

"I'll be seeing you, Bob," he said.

It was the first time I could ever remember him saying my name without bastardizing it.

He walked out the gazebo. He flanked the side of the mortuary and jogged into the darkened cemetery. I watched his lanky frame disappear in the shadows of the night behind some tall gravestones. Two dark shapes appeared behind him, stepping in rhythm. One of them was dragging something. It was odd-shaped and awkward. As I squinted my eyes, I saw it was the body of a dog. A yellow Labrador clutched by the collar with its hind legs and tail dragging in the grass. Just as quickly as they came, they were gone.

It was last time I saw Jacob alive.

CHAPTER SIX:

GREY MATTER

Robert Warrington's Journal
Token-Oak, Winter of 2015
1796 days before the Syndemic

After that trip, my life took a different trajectory. Token-Oak had this way of altering my path. A piece of my determination had broken away. I went back to school, only eight credit hours away from a graduate degree in neuroscience, and I switched to child psychology. My change dumbfounded Postitch. We had spent six years together, often side-by-side in sophisticated research projects turning data points over and over. He didn't understand, and I couldn't explain it. Though, I knew I could not continue the research.

Postitch begged me to stay. He talked about the money and pounded the importance of our study. He kept asking me "why," and I kept telling him I was done. "Why no more brain research… why kids?" He kept repeating the company line that we were on the forefront of medical advances we could potentially save countless human lives.

Sitting on the balcony of his spacious condo overlooking campus, I told him everything. *Everything.* He hugged me like a brother and cried genuine tears, his Sideshow Bob curly afro nearly smothering me to death. Postitch told me a heart-wrenching story about his own escape from family strife. In Israel, he endured molestation and mind-boggling poverty. He worked odd jobs and stole just enough to make it to America. Arriving somewhere in Texas, penniless and alone, he worked for a distant cousin. For many years, the fear of deportation hung over his head like a death sentence. His story was so genuine that I told him I wanted to stay, but he could sense my heart wasn't in it anymore. We parted as good friends.

I called Fran the next morning. She already knew I was leaving though she tried to act disappointed. We talked for only a few minutes, and she closed by reminding me of my promise never to tell another person. "You need to give the money back," Fran said.

"I'll cut you a check in the morning," I blurted.

There was a long pause. Fran had not expected that I wanted out so badly. She paid me for three years up front, and I'd worked a sixth of the time. I'd planned to return the unearned portion without her prompting.

"You don't strike me as a person I have to threaten," she said, "the people I work for don't do nondisclosure agreements. It would be in your best interest to keep this to yourself."

"Fran, I won't discuss it. Ever."

"For your sake," she said, "I hope so. I'll find out if you do. And the response will be out of my hands. And whomever you told would be in a very bad situation." She wished me "good luck," in a tone tantamount to an insult and hung up.

I spent another semester at school. By the time I graduated, I was ready to work with kids. The field of child psychology attracted me. It was more than a calling. Listening to little children explain their problems moved my soul. I went from the promise of saving thousands of human lives to teaching just one child a day the tools to cope with stress. And, to quote Bob Frost, "that made all the difference."

After graduation, I moved from Cambridge to a medium-size Missouri town. I found a teaching Fellowship working with elementary school kids who had anger issues. In a quaint little burg just outside the Ozarks, I rented a tiny apartment above a hardware store on a Main Street. Lakes surrounded the town. There were tall pines everywhere, and the entire place smelled like fresh flowers most mornings. In the evenings, I'd walk with my hands in my pockets down winding paths whistling tunes. All the trees had leaves that didn't clack like brittle bones in high winds.

I found a storefront owned by a retiring probate attorney on Main Street. The place had massive circle windows in the front and a covered porch with a swing. The building cost $500 a month with no deposit. In a week, I'd moved in and hung a shingle out front. I decorated my office with puffy furniture and hundreds of framed photographs from various points in my life. After my first client, I bought the best coffee maker I could afford. In my ample downtime, I sipped world-class joe from ceramic mugs with stupid slogans waving to the locals from my porch.

My work was a joy filled with—and I think Twain said this—"the wonderful mispronunciations of childhood." I had little guys and gals that needed a friend. I spent half my time in my office playing with a Nerf basketball goal or drawing pictures at the arts-and-crafts table.

Two other child phycologists officed within thirty miles of my practice. Money was tight, but, somehow, I always had enough to cover my rent, buy groceries, and spring for good coffee. There were evening walks through the woods, and I even took up fly-fishing in the local streams as a hobby. *Ahh*, it was a life of leisure indeed.

I talked to Grandpa occasionally. He was adjusting to life alone. In the past, he always had someone to service his needs. When he wasn't eating fast food, he was hand scooping Boston cream pies from the local Piggly Wiggly. For lunch, he confessed to a diet of a "soda pop" and a "Zero Bar." And on more than one occasion, he "got by on lemon drops and cups of pudding." It was the survival of the eldest. In a mobile society, where life expectancies had grown long, many elderly people were scraping the bottom of the grease barrel with a used spork from Kentucky Fried Chicken. As a seventy-year-old bachelor, he was floundering.

Summer turned into winter, and Grandpa asked me to come back to Token-Oak for Christmas. He started with a guilt trip by planting little seeds. "Christmas," he said, "such a lonely time. All a man wants is to be surrounded by family. Is that too much to ask? Did I mention how lonely the holiday season can be." I heard him shuffling papers in his office. He believed in the power of the handwritten letter and mailed dozens each week.

"Ever since Grandma died, it's hard on an old man."

He paused, letting out a few exasperated sighs. Those long-winded exhales a person releases when faced with an impossible task.

"You remember, Bob, when I used to give you those hundred dolla…"

"Jesus H. Christ stop it, Gramps. I'll come," I said.

He let out a howl that stretched on for a half minute. A long chuckle culminated with a knee slap. I smiled into the phone.

I asked him when he last saw Jacob, and all the good feelings died. "Yeah, I never see that piece of shit. Doesn't call, doesn't write. He's just disappeared like D.B. Cooper. I see his car though, parked at the base of the Hilltop. I know he's hanging out with those fucking meth freaks. Killing dogs and baking drugs in the woods. Must be one hell of a life. Grandma is rolling over in her grave!"

"Have you tried to talk to him," I said. "Stopped and left him a note on the windshield?"

"A note? What the hell good is that going to do? He's dead, Bob. It's just a matter of time."

I waited a while for Gramps to calm.

"You think you could be here on Christmas Eve?" Grandpa asked. I agreed. When I hung up, I started to regret my promise.

Token-Oak is the place where people never change. No matter how far away a person moves, Token-Oak is still inside them. Driving into the town was like stepping back through time itself. All the way back to when you used to be something lesser. It's true that people never change, but they get better at repressing who they are, submerging it in a vessel deep under the water of time and experience. But all that stuff inside drifts back to the surface when you go home, like the wreckage of a ship at sea. It's a full psychological transformation, a cultural shift, that only escapees from small towns can appreciate.

I thought about Jacob that night with those deep-set eyes. The funeral was only a few years ago, but part of me was itching to get home. It was the same part, I thought, that enticed Token-Oakeans to funerals. It wasn't enough to smell it secondhand from Gramps on the phone, I had to swim in the ether. I thought about the driveway, the pigs, and that night Jacob and I spent together on his roof in between those dead oaks just staring at the Hollows.

After driving eight hours, I turned onto Grandpa's driveway and shifted my car into park. It was one of those strange nights with a huge moon and thin strings of clouds drifting above in swift streams. It felt like the world was moving at an alarming rate. The trees overhead creaked in the wind.

There were no lights on in Grandpa's house save one at the top of the stairs in the kitchen. I got out of my car and popped the trunk to grab my bag and some Christmas presents. As I stepped towards the house, I felt a peculiar sensitivity, a sensation that started in my throat and fell to my stomach as I swallowed the night air. A queasy uneasiness settled over me, an instinct that entering the house was a bad idea.

Out the corner of my eye, I saw an old Buick underneath the pin oak in Grandpa's front yard. It was Jacob's car, all beat to shit. The car had smashed into the tree. Steam sizzled from the radiator. The keys dangled in the ignition and the driver's door was open. The hood was crumpled inward, and there were deep ruts in the yard.

I took a few steps and stopped on the driveway at the exact spot where Jacob and I, twenty years prior, played a game of basketball. And I swear to you, the wind whistled that awful nickname. Subtle at first, like a whisper too soft to catch. As the breeze shifted, I heard it better. The full sound erupted out in the same staccato hiss: Bha-*aab*.

Footsteps squeaked on the driveway, the sound of sneakers twisting on concrete. A few seconds later, the garage door erupted like someone slammed into it. I looked back up at the moon, and the clouds swept past in a slow rumbling order.

The door that lead from the stairs to the kitchen was slightly open. I stopped, looked up at the window Grandma had stood at years ago. Her words, the very words I'd dismissed years prior, came rumbling back in my mind: "I'll be dead, and you'll need him, for what's coming."

There was movement all around me, and it wasn't just the wind. I stood in the open of the driveway surrounded by the rooftops of Grandpa's house and the neighbor's two-story home. I felt exposed, like the air itself collapsed upon me. Footsteps echoed on the street behind me and on the wood shingles from the rooftops above. The rhythm of the steps was a quick patter, and they were everywhere. I heard nasal breathing, the hiss of someone with asthma. Shadows shifted against the side of the garage and on the concrete near my feet. My car was at the end of the driveway, and the kitchen door was just a few feet from where I stood.

I dropped my bag and the presents. I broke into a run. My palms with fingers stretched were parallel with the ground as I ran towards the door. I felt gooseflesh crawl up my spine and wrap around my scalp.

I threw open the kitchen door and jumped inside, slamming it shut behind me. I felt the lock in my hands and snapped it shut. I listened with my ear against the door to the rustling outside.

There was a smell inside the house. It was a pungent odor that burned the tips of nose hairs and singed the lobes of the lungs. Not just any scent, the smolder of freshly discharged gunpowder. My eyes widened, and my heartbeat pounded like a bass drum. My bottom lip quivered so hard my molars clacked.

I walked up the kitchen steps until I reached the top. Just as I was about to yell out for Grandpa, I saw him sitting underneath the single light at the kitchen table. He wore a jacket with the collar pulled up and a baseball cap perched on his head. He was tucked into himself. A violent shiver, a whole-body spasm, made his spectacles shake.

I'd seen Grandpa sit at the table all my life. Usually with his legs crossed, and the newspaper pinched in his index finger, purposefully ignoring the world. He always had this confidence in his chest with his shoulders back. Grandpa was the only man in history who could strut while sitting. But all that machismo was gone. The man I saw before me shook like a homeless drunk on a cold night with a thin jacket. As I inched closer, he was quivering.

"Grandpa?" I said. But he didn't answer or even acknowledge my presence. As I neared him, I saw underneath the bill of his ball cap. There were tears in his eyes, and a resignation stamped into his face. It was like his mind had spilled out on the table before him, and all he could do was watch.

"Grandpa?" I said again, squatting down to his eye level and grabbing his shoulder. But he wouldn't look at me. He stared past me at the blackness at the top of the stairs.

"Grandpa? Grandpa! Hey!" And I shook him with both hands until he realized I was there.

"Jacob's downstairs," he said as he squeezed his eyes. He was sobbing so violently his whole body shook.

I turned towards the stairs and the darkness downward. The steps led down to the back door, then took a sharp left descending into the basement. Right inside the back door—it had been there since I was a little kid—was a picture of Jesus. He was the apotheosis of strength shouldering a massive cross. It was an old oil painting framed in cheap barn wood. There was an ephemeral haze surrounding the Christ that made his head look like it was floating.

Looking into Jesus' eyes, I took the first step into blackness. My knees buckled, and I had to grab the rail for support. I hadn't been in the house in a long time, and I couldn't find the light switch. My feet slithered down the stairs, further into the dark. All the while, my palms ran along the walls searching for the switch. The tips of my fingers probed the wall. I felt something round and hard. After feeling it a moment, I realized it was a plaster plate with the imprint of a set of tiny human hands. Carved into the plate, was the single word "Jacob." I realized I was feeling Jacob's kindergarten plaster of Paris imprints. My hands pulled away from the wall and returned to the rail as I descended more.

I stumbled and slid further down the carpeted steps. My breathing was uneasy as I descended into the darkness. Eventually, my feet reached the flat basement floor. I remembered there was a lamp somewhere nearby, a wagon table lamp maybe. I stuck out my hands like Frankenstein and walked into the black, reaching for the lamp shade. The acrid smell of a discharged firearm was overpowering, and in the deep black of the basement, there was something new. I could taste metal on my tongue like I had a thousand pennies in my mouth. There was a metallic taste intermixing with the burnt odor. This made the hairs on my neck stand up like I had my hands on a plasma globe, the static electricity in the air was so powerful I could have started a fire. I knew Grandpa's office was near.

I felt through the darkness until I found the doorframe to Grandpa's office. I choked on the smell with a pathetic cough. All the while I smacked my mouth to remove the metal taste. As I reached the doorframe, my fingers felt wood in the darkness. I slid my palm across the doorframe that had our childhood heights scrawled into the wood. Muscle memory came then, and I knew there was a light switch on the wall just inside the doorframe.

My fingers fumbled around on the wall, and I felt something warm and wet. I knew it was blood. There was something else mixed in there, something fluffy that felt like cotton balls pulled apart. I slid my hands down the wall and prepared myself for what I was about to see. I found the switch and pinched it in my fingers. I closed my eyes and took a deep breath.

I would like to tell you I approached everything after with stoic silence. That I recorded what followed like Charles Darwin cataloging animals on the Galápagos Islands. None of that is true. I flipped on the light and instantly stopped breathing. From the door of the office, I looked down on the scene. Something inside me grew. Beginning in my stomach, it may have started as a scream. Then it morphed into a childish cry.

Further still, this reaction twisted inside me like a steel braid climbing out my throat. It all culminated in me throwing up on the floor facedown into a pool of blood the size of a living room rug. I was on all fours, palms in the pool, surrounded by white flakes that were the texture of calamari.

I crouched before Grandpa's desk on all fours in a pool of blood and brains. My eyes slammed shut for a long time. I thought about the laboratory all the way back in undergrad. I'd spent countless hours pulling microscopic cross-sections of brains onto glass slides. I'd stare into the nether regions of a cross-section through a microscope, searching for clues about neuroplasticity. It was all demon teeth and butterflies. The thought came then as I looked at the blood on my hands and the white specks of grey matter speckled along my arms and palms. I was the red rat. My whole life had been one big experiment, a prolonged exercise in self-immolation and the effects of stress on the brain. My returns to Token-Oak were the experimental copulation before someone grabbed me from the thresher and guillotined my head off. For the briefest of moments, I looked at the gun and understood what happened. The thought occurred that "I was slipping away." So, I shook my head and took a deep breath.

I peered over the desk. The choking smell of burnt gunpowder hung heavy in the air. There was a hole in the ceiling above the counter and a bullpup shotgun laying on the floor. I spent enough time on the farm to know it was heavy buckshot. It did its job, too.

Jacob was still sitting in Grandpa's wingback chair. The top of his head was completely blown off. Only a jagged part of his forehead remained. Jacob's eyes were still open, and that same deep-thinking-troubled-artist stare he'd worked so hard to perfect as a child was forever chiseled into his face. There was this crooked circle in his lip where the shotgun barrel protruded before it hit the floor. One thing they don't tell you in the movies is people that shoot themselves also shit themselves. If there's enough blood in the room, you can taste the metal. As I looked into Jacob's eyes, those postured eyes, the smell of metal and shit spun through my nose.

A feeling settled over me that wasn't quite resignation or calmness. It was an understanding. As I breathed in the brains and the blood, I knew where I was and where I was headed. I spent six years removing brains and slicing them into a thousand pieces. As I looked around Grandpa's office, at the glass desk with family photos beneath, it was just like looking at a slide in the lab. There was a palpable sense that everything that had happened— maybe even all the way back to the pigs—led to this moment.

Jacob had walked into Grandpa's office on Christmas Eve. He took a bullpup shotgun off the wall, loaded it with double-aught buckshot, put the barrel in his mouth, and pulled the trigger. On Christmas fucking Eve. Some people go to the woods, take a bottle of pills, or drive their car at top speed into an embankment. Jacob went into his grandfather's most treasured place and spread parts of himself throughout the room.

I looked back at Jacob. He sat in the chair still staring forward. For the first time, I noticed Jacob was emaciated. The skin on his neck and arms hung off him like a wrinkled sheet. Even though his face was covered with blood, I saw the rings around his eye sockets cut deep into his face like finely wrought tattoos. He was dressed in clothes so dirty and black I couldn't even tell the fabric. It was clear, for the first time, he had become one of them. He was part of the Hollows. He was one of the few that made his way back. Even if only for a few moments before shooting himself, Jacob had made it home.

I realized Grandpa was still upstairs, sitting at the kitchen table. My hands were covered in blood, and there wasn't a sink in the basement. There was a sweatshirt on the back of the chair where Jacob sat. I took a step towards him to grab the sweatshirt and, as I did, something in the room shifted. Couldn't be from the floor because the floor was concrete. I didn't kick the desk or touch the chair. As I approached, the chair rolled slightly, and Jacob's body slid toward me. Tilting first to the right side and correcting itself as it leaned forward and down. Jacob collapsed on the floor. What remained of his brain spilled out onto the carpet. I stood there for another minute looking down.

Jacob was left sitting Indian-style, the way he slumped out of the chair with his head down. His brain stem held the remainder of his brain in his skull. There were a million ways he could've come to rest spilling out of the chair. That was Token-Oak, the town of grotesque coincidences. I wiped my hands on the sweatshirt and went upstairs to talk to Grandpa.

I called the police as the sun came up through the kitchen window. It was the most radiant sunrise I could ever remember. The clouds splashed the sky with brilliant reds and pink. Grandpa and I sat on the porch, waiting for the police to arrive, staring up at the morning sky. Grandpa didn't say a word all morning.

I helped plan the funeral and coordinate the cleanup which the home insurance covered. A cleaning contractor unit ripped out the carpet and replaced the ceiling tiles. When they were gone, an odd pattern of bright white tiles was juxtaposed with several tiles stained from decades of grime. It served as a reminder of what happened, of just how messy life had become.

I caught Grandpa staring at it once. He was underneath the white shape, right where the double-aught buckshot passed through the ceiling. He said that must be the place where Jacob "ascended into heaven." His tone tickled the lie. I didn't believe in hell, not back then at least. I knew if there were a hell, Jacob would be there selling people suntan lotion and heat suits at a 400 percent markup.

Jacob's funeral was attended by three people that cared. The rest of Token-Oak came to gawk. There was no eulogy, just a sermon from a pastor that knew Jacob when he was a little boy. He spoke about God throwing a rope to Jacob and pulling him into heaven. The silver casket sat closed before him as he threw out clichés about the afterlife. I heard a middle-aged woman whisper to her husband that "suicides don't go to heaven." I left the mortuary thinking about Jacob being stuck in the basement for eternity.

Grandpa was alone after the funeral, and it was hard to leave him. He claimed he was all right. A few times he asked me to leave, but I could tell he didn't want me to go. Eventually, I had obligations piling, and I had no choice but to return to my life.

When I drove out of Token-Oak, through the twisting two lanes and barbed wire, I planned to never go back. Grandpa, I thought, would get old enough that he would have to leave. There was nothing left for me in that place but bad memories. Even as I left, all I could hear was the rustling of the dead trees in a high wind. The dehydrated branches clacking together like skeletons. Turns out old memories die hard. Bad memories live on forever and can reach across time and space.

CHAPTER SEVEN:

FOR OLD TIME'S SAKE

Robert Warrington's Journal
Hannibal, Missouri, October 2020
5 days before the Syndemic

I went back to my small town and continued to practice. It was a hard slog, especially at first. I spent months sleeping in my office and bathing out of the bathroom sink. After a few years of dodging creditors, my business gelled. I moved from the hardware store location to a little office on Main Street.

A few years passed, and my thirties approached like a distant mountain. Finally, I'd found my calling, and that made a difference. The kids made work easy. Listening to a five-year-old describe a delicate emotional situation warmed my heart. One of the other child psychologists in my little town retired, and I picked up a government contract for Medicaid clients with troubled kids. That kept the lights on and even provided enough scratch for me to rent a decent apartment. In the evenings, I spoke about depression at local schools around the region. It was fulfilling work and, three years in, I turned a healthy profit.

After one particularly successful month, I had a nice cushion in my operating account. The speaking engagements paid off. I hired a staff and dropped twenty thousand on a modern filing system. Parents drove their kids from neighboring states. Moderate success—a single secretary and two computers—developed into a thriving venture, a second psychologist, a filing clerk, and a phalanx of computers tied to a server. My hours got longer, and I spent entire nights at the office. But the work was my passion, and I'd do anything to accommodate a patient.

Postitch came down for a visit one summer. He needed to get away from the lab; he said on the phone, "if only for a week." We walked around Hannibal shops like tourists and had waffle cones of frozen yogurt on the plaza. One night, while sitting around a metal fire pit in my backyard sipping Coors' yellow bellies, he spoke about the research.

"The money will be worth it, you know . . . in the end," he said.

"How is the research going?" I asked.

Postitch looked around the outside of my house and ran his palms down the sides of his pants. He asked me where his phone was, and I said he left it inside on the kitchen table. He looked relieved at this and spent a long time looking across the street at parked cars. After careful consideration, he nodded twice. He was skittish, like a deer in the forest listening to the sounds of cracking sticks. He mumbled something inaudible.

"What?" I said.

"You ever float the river," he said louder.

I told him that kids go on float trips all the time. In fact, in Missouri, drinking cheap beer and urinating on yourself in an inner tube was a pseudo rite of passage.

"No," he interjected, "I am talking about *the river*. The Mississippi."

"I don't know. I mean commercial tugs are out there all day churning the water. It's a quick-moving river, too. So, an experienced boater could do it. I guess."

"Do we dare? Let's leave our phones behind and head out onto the muddy beast. Like Lewis and Clark. Like Frodo and Samwise going into Mordor." He smiled big, and the locks of his curly afro shook as he laughed.

In the morning, we drove to the local Wal-Mart and bought a canoe and two wooden paddles. An hour after stocking a cooler full of beer and food, we were standing on the banks of the great river. Watching boats the size of football stadiums putter past. Postitch waded out, and we both hopped in the boat. The current of the river swept us away.

We floated for eight hours, sipping beers and waving at commercial tugs and tourist steamboats alike. Once we were forty miles downstream and in the middle of the open river, Postitch steered the canoe onto the banks of an island in the middle of the river. We pulled the boat ashore and grilled hotdogs over an impromptu campfire.

"The research has taken a turn," he whispered as he rolled the soft white bread of his hotdog over in his hands. Even out in the middle of nowhere, he was still cautious. "The best I can tell, the agency running the study is a mixture of NSA and the CDC. And they're studying addiction, all right. But they seem more interested in understanding addiction contagion."

"What the hell is that?

"You remember the researcher that studied suicide clusters? That, in schools, communities, social networks… one suicide will lead to a rash of others? Well, that is contagion. *Suicide contagion…* it's all psychological. There—and I am no expert on this, all right?—are specific factors that lead to such a contagion. It seems the government wants to understand addiction contagion if there is such a thing. Is addiction itself a vehicle for contagion?"

"What is the usefulness of that?"

"If you understand the factors that lead to such a contagion, you could cripple a country. Or, if you understood the triggers, you could prevent the spread of addiction at home. We're talking billions and billions of dollars here. Can you imagine this in the hands of big Pharma? They'd break the bank for this knowledge, right?"

"Did you ever find out where they are getting the samples? Did you ever find out about the smell?

Postitch nodded. "I did."

"You did?"

He nodded again.

I waited. For the next few minutes, we sat in the woods of the island watching the fire crackle as I fed new twigs and little branches into the pile. He thought about what to say for a long time.

"Those samples," he said, "come from live studies all over the country. They're running multiple controls in at least ten different towns and cities. All these people are overdosing, and they're just letting it happen. At least, I think they're ODing—hell, I they could be just killing junkies in cold blood. They test each group with different triggers, and different drugs, and different delivery systems. Eventually, they will find a combination."

"Delivery systems? Like what?

"I can only guess, but they would put chemicals into anything people ingest: water, air, food, drugs… take your pick."

"*Jesus.*"

"Yeah," Postitch said, "it's not the shit I wanted to do with my degree." He spent a half hour, near tears, telling me about his emotional struggles. Addiction, and treating addicts was why he got involved in the research. It was all so dehumanizing, so calculated, the way the government was studying the addiction pathology.

"Where are these field studies—these towns where they are pulling samples—located?"

"I don't know," he said and stirred the fire with a stick. "I've been thinking about my family farm. Thinking about going back, working the ground, putting up new homes, and providing for my people. I send them a few thousand bucks every month. But what I know now is I'll never be able to leave that place. If I pulled all that money out and tried to jump on a plane, I'd get stopped before I left the bank parking lot."

"You don't know that," I said. "They let me go just fine."

"They let you go because they had me. They let you go because the research needed to go on. But when it ends... *when it ends*." Postitch just shook his head and threw the rest of the sticks onto the fire.

The sun was dipping into the tips of the trees. The sound of the Mississippi roared around us. There were crickets in the woods and the cryptic buzzing of locusts whining over the water like planes running out of gas. A realization set in that we would have to head back into the water and out onto the furious current during the darkness. The woods felt ominous then. Long shadows crept across the underbrush like the fingers of a ghastly sadness. I rose, and Postitch asked me to sit.

"Just sit here with me for ten more minutes," he said in a yearning voice. "Please."

I wanted to tell him we had to go. That boarding the boat in the dark would be dangerous. That we needed to go just to spot a safe place on the far bank to get out of the river. But, somehow, I felt he needed to sit in those woods just a little longer.

About three years in, I had a client, Isabella, who worked as a traveling nurse and struggled with her eleven-year-old son, Alejandro. No other child psychologist would meet with her. The few that tried found "Alex" so belligerent they refused a second session. Isabella had only one-half day off a week, usually on Saturday nights, so scheduling her was difficult. After a few reschedules, and a missed appointment, we found time on a weekend.

In the week prior, Alex allegedly stabbed a classmate with a sharpened pencil. He hit an artery and caused nerve damage. There was a civil suit filed, and the parents of the injured child wanted Alex suspended indefinitely. The juvenile court judge ordered a psychological evaluation before deciding.

The two previous psychologists failed to connect with Alex. As Isabella explained it, there was always a wall, an impenetrable barrier no one could break. She was frantically trying to help Alex because she felt if she didn't resolve these issues before middle school, Alex was headed for "a lonely place."

There was a genuine motherly instinct in Isabella. After a few years of practice, you develop an ability to separate the parents that: (1) love their kids and want to help, from (2) those that just go through the motions. Alex's mom gave everything she had to "make him better." It wasn't enough. As a result, he was backsliding, and she was losing her grip on life. Her love for Alex was so unalloyed; her tears of concern were so genuine that it made my heart hurt just to listen to her breathe on the phone.

On a dreary October evening, I met Alex. A hard, wet wind blew freezing rain. Isabella and Alex appeared in my foyer just past seven p.m. wearing parkas and boots. Alex had jet-black hair pulled back into a ponytail. He had his mother's attractive features, piercing eyes that ambled from one thing to the next. His head stayed still as his eyes glided over everything in my office. Alex spoke very little. Instead he shook his head either "yes" or "no," and even that was so subtle I could barely decide which one. He pursed his lips together as if he was angry at the world. There was something inside him, a yearning to connect that was buried underneath a calculated exterior. If I could peel back the layers, I thought, I could help.

The first session I met with Alejandro and Isabella. I knew instantly this was a mistake. Most of our two hours involved Alex and his mom cussing at each other in a biting Spanish dialect. My Spanish was weak, but I understood emotions. I could decipher the gist of their conversations. A resilient child, and, headed into the world with his chin down and one shoulder forward. To his adolescent mind, everything was a slog. He wore a deep-seated distrust of adults like a pair of shackles. After two hours of struggle, I sent them home disappointed.

On our second session, I asked to see Alex alone. My initial questions were softballs and open-ended: "what are your hobbies?" "what makes you happy?" "if you could do anything, what would you do?" To say Alex was reticent was an understatement. I filled the silence with thoughts that came from his appearance. He wore basketball shoes that looked both expensive and carefully selected. The type of shoes probably named after a player: Curry, Durant, or Lebron. I started talking about b-ball. The eternal debate: Jordan—with his six titles—or Lebron—with his ungodly size and athleticism. This was a desperate attempt at a connection, and Alex saw right through it. But it cracked the door a little.

He had a Teenage Mutant Ninja Turtles backpack, and I told him I used to watch the cartoon when I was a little kid.

"*Every* Saturday I would sit in front of the tube with a mixing bowl full of Peanut Butter Crunch and watch Raphael work people over with his nunchucks," I said a little too cheerfully.

"Michelangelo had the 'chuks, Raphael had a sai," he said. He looked away from me and resumed his silence. He sat on my couch examining things in my room. His head barely moved, but his eyes danced from one item to the next. He looked at all my pictures one by one. Alex methodically read the titles of the books on my shelf. Alex spoke so little, I had to guess what he was looking at to make conversation. Several times, I mentioned the title of a book and discussed the characters. Alex closed his eyes and shook his head while blowing air out of his nose in an exasperated chuckle.

After about forty-five minutes of this, I cracked. I broke the cardinal rule of counseling children: I showed a slight frustration in my tone and approach. "Alex, what would you like to talk about." I sat the pen and legal pad on the table between us.

Then the session changed.

He stopped staring at things in my office and looked directly at me. There was a crooked smirk on his face. Like everything, he had done for the past forty-five minutes built to this impasse. He'd gotten to me, and he knew it.

"Robert J. Warrington, M.D.?" Alex said. "That's you?"

"Ph.D., but yeah, that is me," I said while continuing to make eye contact.

For the first time in the session, he held my stare. Alex had a habit of looking, yet not looking directly at a person.

"So, I bet people call you *Bob*?" he said in a sardonic tone. He smiled and chuckled to himself. "*Bob*?" He chortled audibly now and shook his head. With the conversation growing, I moved into a little deeper water.

"Alex, you had trouble at school a few weeks ago. A kid got hurt pretty bad. Do you want to talk about what happened?"

"No, Bob. I don't." And he threw up another wall. As I continued to probe, the questions themselves angered him. I sensed a change inside this eleven-year-old boy sitting on my couch. There was a fury building within him. A deepening resentment that came from somewhere else. Most kids would fold their arms and deflect questions childishly. Some would cover their ears or cry. But Alex sneered at me with slow-moving eyes. He kept repeating my name to himself—Bob, Bob, *Bob*—and nodding his head. Finally, he arched his back on my couch and whistled. We had a two-hour session, so I continued to probe and try to find an opening. I searched hard for common ground, but this angered him more.

As if commanded, Alex slid off the couch and on the floor. He folded his legs into each other and sat Indian style. Or, as the politically correct people say in the schools, I visit, crisscross applesauce. He held his head in his hands and stared at the floor. And he whispered, but it was a whisper that was almost a yell, my nickname in two syllables: "Doctor Bha-*aab*, *I love therapy.*"

Perhaps it was the way he said it or the tone of voice with him sitting there Indian style. Maybe it was the smirk, or the angle of his head tilted slightly to the left. Those combinations of things hit me hard and all at once. I stopped talking, quit probing, my mouth fell open, and the silence of recognition settled over me like mustard gas. I'd seen this all before, ten thousand times. This image lived in my memories. Alex, it seemed, climbed inside my head and pulled this memory to life.

I knew that Alex saw the look on my face. My jaw slammed shut, and I turned away to grab a drink of water before continuing. The air in the room became a little thicker. It felt warm, and a discomfort twisted in my joints like debilitating arthritis.

"You scared?" he said.

"*What?*" I said way too fast and in a high-pitched voice.

"You want to know my hobbies, don't you?"

He paused a long while looking into me. Finally, he said, "I like to scare. I like that 'O-shit' look on your face."

"What look?" I said, trying to play it off.

Alex didn't respond to that comment. He stood up and gave me a smirk that was so coolly contemptuous I gulped.

"Scaring makes me warm. It feels good. It lasts a long time."

I collected myself, shook my head, and grabbed my notepad. I tried to reassert control of the conversation.

"What do you like about it, Alex?"

Alex looked at me without speaking with a mature stare, one that seemed far too cold and sophisticated for an eleven-year-old boy.

Right before I spoke, Alex said "People remember a good scare. Forever. You know what I mean, Dr. Bha-*aab*?" Alex walked around my office.

Every time I looked at him, I saw Jacob as a child, like he was standing in my office, in the flesh. Alex walked around my room and picked up frames. He stood before a framed article of my research project with Postitch and read every word. All the while, he kept mouthing that terrible nickname: "*Bha-aab*." I felt all the torment and ridicule from those long-ago days. Some things were more than run-of-the-mill mannerisms of a sadistic eleven-year-old. The way Alex slid off that couch and onto the floor. The way his head hung down off his neck like he was dead weight. That pose was exceptionally unique, yet I saw it in my office as if transported back to the basement of my grandpa's office. An image came to me, something from long ago. I thought about the Hilltop, the bald rock surface surrounded by those snarling dead oaks. I saw all those piles of rocks spread throughout like mini craters on the moon.

From outside my office window, I heard the wind pick up. The tips of the trees were swishing violently. Riding through that sound was a clacking panic. The banging of dead limbs rode on the breeze, traveling hundreds of miles from Token-Oak. I could even smell the blood from the slaughterhouse and hear the cries of the cattle being shuffled through the feedlots.

I didn't say another word to Alex. The remaining ten minutes clicked away in painful seconds while he stood looking at me. When his mom opened the door to my office, something in Alex changed, and he returned to the couch rubbing his temples.

When Isabella asked how things went, I shook my head and covered my mouth with a palm. My eyes were full of tears, and all I could get out was a half-murmured apology. "I'm sorry," I said, "I tried." She slammed the door so hard leaving my office it knocked one of my diplomas off the wall.

A cruel reality of small-town practice began that night. The same gossip circuit that brought in new clients would work against me. Within the next week, Isabella told everyone at the local hospital I was a step beneath a snake oil salesman. It wouldn't be long, and the whole damn town would know about my misstep.

That night, I locked the door to my office and walked to my apartment a few blocks away. I had a short trip through the park across the street and down a winding hill. My apartment steps were at the edge of a long rock wall. Across the street from those steps was a forest of tall pine and a trailhead to a five-mile hike I'd walked a hundred times. At night, I always looked over to the tip of the trail. It was a beautiful tableau as the path stretched up a hillside for a half mile, and the trees touched over the top of it making an evergreen tunnel. Some nights, you could catch the moon sitting above the trail. It was picturesque in a way that was spooky and welcoming at the same time.

I paused at the bottom of the stairs and looked at the trail. And at the tip, underneath one pine, there was a pile I'd never seen before. As I looked closer, I saw it was two shapes, one laid on top of the other. I took a full minute to realize I saw the outline of two dogs. Someone cut their collars off and put them on the ground. The dogs' fur was matted with dried blood. They were not moving.

I brought my hand to my mouth. There was a memory of something from my past, but I remembered this only vaguely. My hands went numb, and I could not pull air into my lungs. More than anything, the need to get inside overcame me.

That night, I laid on my mattress listening to the rubber tires of cars outside and the ghostly popping of my refrigerator condenser. Sleep was an impossibility. I ran over everything—Alex, Jacob's suicide, the dead dogs— a hundred times. What made Alex say that name and slouch into that posture. Everything about him for half an hour was a carbon copy of my past. He knew things about me that were unknowable. He conjured secrets I didn't even tell myself.

As the weeks passed, I rationalized the moment and grasping at theories. Maybe he somehow channeled my memories? There were ultra-sensitive kids, those that could intuit thoughts from others. There was a burgeoning group of psychologists—of course, they were outcasts because it was scientific nonsense—that believed that very thing. A Harvard dropout that blogged about indigo kids. Claiming that blonde-haired, blue-eyed children had a propensity to read minds and, in exceptional cases, transport emotions to others. But what terrified me was the thought that what I saw and felt in that room wasn't Alex at all. Rather, it was someone else reaching inside him. I didn't know then who was capable of such a thing, but I knew where they were. There was only one place in the world that killed dogs and controlled adolescent kids. It wanted me to know I was being watched.

———————

I struggled in sessions with other kids. The relaxing tone and positive nature I worked for years to develop were the first to go. I got these awful thoughts that overpowered my senses. There was a deluge of "what ifs" and "why me." My mind became a parade of horribles, and I overanalyzed everything. The fear became so palpable it manifested in uncontrollable shakes and panic attacks.

One day, in the middle of a session, a child told me I looked like I was scared to death. The mother confronted me about it, demanding answers. She kept asking me if I was OK and telling me how critical it was that I "provide a place of comfort." As if I didn't understand that was important. After a while, I realized she wasn't worried about me, she thought I was on drugs. She left my office in a rush, and I fully expected a complaint and investigation from the state board.

That night, when I got home, I cracked open a bottle of single malt. I wasn't a big drinker, but on rare occasions, I liked to have a few fingers of smooth whiskey to nurse. On good nights, I'd smoke a cigar on my back porch while pulling sips. But that porch overlooked the trail, and that view had lost its comfort.

This night was different. I cracked open a bottle and filled a water glass. I didn't go outside, I stood in my kitchen, looking through the Venetian blinds at all the passing cars with suspicion. The trailhead was empty, and a hunter's moon hung bathing the trail in a luminescent glow.

There was only one person in the world that would understand my issues. Even though he wouldn't want to share. He spent most of his life ignoring all the weird shit around him. As I stood looking out the window, I called Grandpa. I listened as the phone connection crackled as it connected into the town of Token-Oak. In the millisecond before contact, I heard the hellish transmission sounds of a wireless signal bouncing across the unknown.

CHAPTER EIGHT:

THE GHOSTS OF BHA-AAB

Robert Warrington's Journal
Token-Oak, October 2020
O days before the Syndemic

On that trip back to Token-Oak, I drove in the night. Always down the same two-lane highway cutting through farms going broke and abandoned buildings. It was a countryside wasteland to Token-Oak. A begotten region of America that had a great century during the times of the Indian and the horse. On those lonely roads, the stereo crackled with static every half hour grasping at invisible lines floating in the night sky, occasionally hooking a sermon, a farm store advertisement for seed sale, or a heart-pounding riff of Conway Twitty.

When I was within one hundred miles of Token-Oak, I picked up KXLT 810, the "Buckle," Token-Oak's premiere music station. As a youth, I spent long hours on the tractor, and I had to choose between a Christian call-in station and the Buckle, often going for the latter. I tuned there out of habit, I guess, maybe even a little nostalgia.

As I climbed a gentle rise on a prairie highway that twisted along the tops of several hills, the Buckle burst to life. A modern bluegrass tune wound down and a grizzled, country voice as flat as a pool table, announced the news. "We haven't confirmed it yet, but—ah—there's been an accident along the interstate. A group of people were trying to cross, and eight was hit."

"Eight people hit... on the interstate?" a woman's voice responded.

"It says eight hit, and... the Token-Oak county sheriff is—on—the—scene."

"Oh my, Jimmy, that is terrible," the woman's voice responded.

There was the ruffling of papers and the muffled sound of the DJ covering the microphone.

"There is something else, Darlene," the man named Jimmy said—more papers ruffled, and there was shouting in the background.

"I'm not reporting that, it's wrong," Jimmy said.

"I've got my police scanner on and have a call into Token-Oak Memorial Hospital. They have admitted two hundred people with some kind of sickness. Jimmy, the hospital is busier than hell and bejesus right now... and reports are comin' across now about fifty people..."

"Look, Darlene, let's get this confirmed," Jimmy said sharply. "For a town this small, those numbers can't be right..."

"Can you at least warn those listening about the causes? Confirmed or not, it's the right thing to do," Darlene said.

"I guess we can do that... Listen, there are some unconfirmed reports about overdoses in Token-Oak. If you are listening to this, please note—and we will confirm this shortly—there are reports of—ah—people using IV drugs. The kind you inject. There are reports that—ah—several have been rushed to the hospital in the last hour. Rethink the drug use and be careful. People are getting hurt. Even worse. Is that good, Darlene?"

"Thanks for listening to the Buckle," said Darlene. There was dead air for about fifteen seconds before the same set of commercials recycled. I reached over and switched the radio off. I drove through the undulations in the Smoky Hills on my way to Token-Oak.

———————

"I still smell it, you know," Grandpa said. The old man was talking about the formaldehyde the crime scene clean-up team used to remove the blood from the basement after Jacob's suicide. He shifted in his seat as if he was about to unburden himself from a great weight.

"It's in my clothes. Hell, sometimes I taste it in the food. I guess it's his parting gift to the world, the formaldehyde lingering. I can't believe he went down to my office and shot himself on Christmas Eve." Grandpa shook his head and breathed deep. There was something in his face I couldn't quite place. He shut his eyes slowly and kept them closed for a few seconds. Then he reached out and grabbed my knee, said how much he appreciated me "coming down on short notice."

We were sitting in the kitchen on a fall afternoon. Snow had accumulated on the porch outside. I made us both a fresh cup of coffee. We sipped our mugs and stared at the falling flakes. It was that stage of snow where a fresh powder covered everything, before time and temperature eroded the beauty.

"Weatherman says this is the earliest snowfall in Kansas history," said Gramps. He sipped from his mug and watched the flakes fall in fat feathers.

Gramps was never the same after losing his wife and grandson in the same year. His eyes darted around, and he had the new habit of biting his bottom lip to prevent it from trembling. There was an alien emotion inside him, digging around the sides of his face. I took a while to realize what I was seeing was fear. There was a long silence as I watched him stare outside. Gramps watched the rooftop of his neighbor's house like he was expecting something to happen. His breathing was irregular, and he kept running his thumb over his knuckles.

"What is it, Gramps?" I said. He said nothing for a few minutes and went back to reading his agricultural magazine. I sat in silence, in the old house, watching the snow fall.

We talked that night—and I mean communicated about life outside of sports and politics—for the first time in a while. Gramps repeated himself and subtly shook. Whenever he got confused, which was often, he took short breaths. But he unloaded a lot in only a few hours. The conversation was a hard schlep uphill.

We talked about Grandma and what a great woman she was. He danced around her quirks. Like how she refused to leave the house at night, and how much she hated living in Token-Oak, yet she never left. We talked about the farm and, unavoidably, about the great underdog sports battles going on in the world right now. There was one subject he didn't go into, that was Jacob. But it sat there on the edge of his tongue, like a gargoyle perched on the side of the building. Sure, he talked about the smell and the way his office was never the same. Though, he did not talk about Jacob.

As day turned into night, we made bologna sandwiches from white bread with Miracle Whip. We had a small mountain of Ruffles chips on white paper plates with cans of warm Dr. Pepper. For dessert, we ate ice cream sandwiches that had freezer burn so bad they cracked when bitten. Gramps was living the bachelor lifestyle, and his diet was pure shit.

Just after ten o'clock, Grandpa told me about the "sleeping arrangements." In the past few months, he had sold or given away most of the house furniture. The guest room bed and the twin beds upstairs were gone.

"You can either make a pallet on the floor in the guest room or sleep on the divan in the basement," he said.

There was something inside me, a little whisper, not quite my subconscious, but something behind my memories that said simply: *sleep in the basement*. That was, as I realized sitting in that kitchen, the reason I came back. *He* was down there, I could feel it in my bones as I thought about the suicide. Jacob was in that basement, and I was going to find him.

Before Grandpa went to bed, he brought in a ceramic turkey and sat it on the table. It was two-feet tall; the bottle sat on the top shelf of Grandpa's office ever since I was a little kid. It was a decanter full of whiskey, and not just any whiskey. It had *Wild Turkey* sloshing inside its glass feathers. There were few things Grandpa treasured, and the sharp taste of Wild Turkey was one. Grandpa pulled the head off the glass bird with a comical pop. The pungent odors of charred wood and butterscotch filled the room. Grandpa always called Wild Turkey "swamp" because of the way it made him think. We shared a glass and talked about the "good old days."

Grandpa had this habit of taking big gulps of whiskey with a huge smile on his face. It made him a fun drinking partner. He'd pound down a gulp then tell a story. After two glasses, the stories became performances. Show tunes like "Camp Town Races" and lonesome poems. After three glasses of "swamp," Gramps tried to recite Whitman's "O' Captain, My Captain" in a maudlin tone:

"My Captain does not answer, his lips are pale and still,

My father does not feel my arm, he has no pulse nor will,

The ship is anchor'd safe and sound, its voyage closed and done,

From fearful trip the victor ship comes in with object won;

Exult O shores, and ring O bells!

But I with mournful tread,

Walk the deck my Captain lies,

Fallen cold and dead."

The last refrain stalled him. His eyebrows furrowed, and he lowered his head. He nodded softly, then rose from the table, leaving the words of Whitman to hang between us. Gramps patted my shoulder and stumbled to his bedroom. The door shut behind him with a *thwomp*.

I sat in the house, alone. The galley kitchen smothered around the tiny table. Grandma's bric-à-brac was still speckled throughout. Everything was untouched from my childhood. Two dozen owls were staring back at me.

Something drew my eyes to the dirty sunflower linoleum spot where Grandma died. For some reason, I thought about roadside graves. How loved ones left flowers and vigils on the sides of dirty highways in the very spot where people passed. It seemed people just understood the place a person died held importance. I wondered, staring into the yellow geometry of a faded flower, if Grandma remained in that area.

Grandma had called me back. It wasn't Token-Oak, a guilty conscience, or the fact my life was falling apart that brought me home. It was her. She was gone but still around, at least some part of her. If there was a woman that could reach across the Great Divide, my grandmother could do it. And then I knew, staring into the dirty sunflower on the floor, she wanted me to go into the basement. She'd been warning me about what was about to happen for years.

Just a few feet beyond that spot was the blackness at the top of the stairs leading into the basement. Down those twisting steps, in the office at the bottom, was the last spot Jacob occupied in this world. If there was any truth to roadside graves if those that died in the twisting metal coffins haunted highways long after death, if flowers and mementos left by loved ones were touched by the fingers of deceased specters, then Jacob was still there. All the formaldehyde and alcohol swabs rubbed in by the crime scene people could not erase his being.

I stood at the kitchen table, the chair legs squealed as it slid backward. I gulped, but my throat was dry.

My phone vibrated in my front pocket. Deep in thought, I twitched backward to pull it free. It was an unknown number, a caller ID not listed. I never answered calls from people I didn't know, but this felt different. I held the phone to my ear while I stared into the darkness of the basement.

There was a strange, humming echo. I heard the ruffle of clothes and what sounded like a box fan. A desperate whisper, barely audible over the noise, hissed into the phone.

"Are you there?"

"Who is this?" I said sternly.

"Postitch." There was more shuffling and then a loud bang followed by Yiddish cursing.

"Postitch? Why the hell are you whispering? What's going on?

"I don't have a lot of time... remember our conversation a few months back on the island?

"I remember."

"They solved the riddle of contagion, but it's fucked. They've been focusing on a rural area in the middle of nowhere. Some backwater eddy that is overrun with addiction. They've been putting poisons and psychotropics into fertilizers there for years. Almost every sample we get comes from the same area. It's not even a town. Just some spot about a few miles outside of a little place called Token-Oak in a set of hills."

There was a muffled sound and heavy breathing. The phone went silent for nearly a half minute.

"Postitch?" I finally said.

"Yeah, I'm here. Listen, this could get worse. There are things they didn't expect. Apparently, this dope manufactured in this rural spot has been shipped all over the nation. It's everywhere. They have a map up in the conference room of hot spots. Also, they did not expect the impact of mixing with other drugs. The overdoses of this will be astronomical. And these addicts, they…"

There was more muffled sounds and another long pause.

"I'll call soon if I can. In the meantime, get the hell out of Missouri. You are too close to this thing. The fallout from this will be huge. It will overrun entire states in the Midwest with this shit…"

"What happens with the addicts?"

"They overdose, but their brain doesn't die. Not all of it, anyway. What's left just takes over. It all comes from IV drug use. Something happens to the chemical when heated and mixed. There could be fifty thousand addicts out there. Maybe more."

"What are you going to do?"

"I'm bugging out. I have a storage unit in Chicago just south of town. There are tons of supplies and food. Once I grab that, I'm headed to the Rocky Mountains. My uncle has a ranch in Colorado. You could meet me there. Better yet, meet me at Scotts Bluff in Nebraska. I'll camp in the lower basin north of the highest bluff for a few weeks. Can you do it?"

"I can. Can we meet there in three weeks?"

"Yeah, I'll wait for you as long as I can north of the Bluffs. Cell service may collapse. This may be the last time we talk for a while."

"I'll be there."

"One more thing, be careful of kids. There is something about the chemical interaction and the adolescent brain.

"Be careful, how?"

The phone went silent. The loud ruffling of clothing smothered the line. Then the connection clicked off to a dial tone.

———————————————

I stood at the top of the basement stairs. I remember the day Jacob shot himself and the eyes of Jesus at the top of the blackness. Most of all, though, I remembered my fingertips feeling into the dark. My hands tingled again at the memory. The way my fingers slid across the blood to find that switch danced in my mind. My sphincter tightened, and my eyes widened with each step downward.

I made it to the bottom. To my left was Grandpa's office. To my right, was the basement living room. I walked over to the office door and found the light switch. Right before the light came on, I stood in the darkness and closed my eyes. I took a breath so deep that my chest arched forward, then I closed my eyes and stood perfectly still. I didn't blink or move for a full minute.

A defining quiet blanketed the room. It was so quiet, except for the faint sound of the radiator upstairs and the sawing of crickets in the garage. I noticed the air itself was still. There are few places in modern life were still air and perfect quiet combine. As I stood, the hairs on the back of my neck rose. I spread my arms out into the dark room. With my eyes closed, I opened up to Jacob. I wanted him to be there. I needed him to be there.

For minutes, I heard nothing except the sound of my own breath and the beating of my panicked heart. I stood there in the stillness like a penitent parishioner praying for a sign. I eventually gave up and turned on the light of the office. The tingle in my spine loosened its grip.

The office looked eerily familiar. The carpet was new, and there were a few clean ceiling tiles. Jacob shot himself with the double-aught buckshot, which passed up through his skull, through the top of the ceiling into the kitchen, destroying several tiles in its wake. Everything else was the same. There were blood stains on picture frames and on the lampshade. A person had died in that room, but nothing had changed. I was shocked that Grandpa didn't throw everything away.

I sat in Grandpa's office chair for a long time. My eyes wandering from one trinket to the next. My mind replayed that night. I'd worked so hard not to think about Jacob. Token-Oak itself was always relegated to a dark corner of my mind. For the first time, maybe ever, I summoned forth all those repressed memories. There was a conscious effort to relive, to revive. My life was falling apart, and I'd come back searching for the answer. There was a feeling I'd find what I was looking for was in the room.

Minutes passed again, there was nothing except the sound of my own breath. I sighed deeply and stood. Before I shut off the light, I stopped one last time and waited. Nothing came, and I left the office. My disappointment trailing behind me like the rooster tail of a pick-up truck on a dirt road.

I walked into the basement living room and stretched out on the divan. I laid down a pillow and a bottom sheet across the couch. I pulled a quilt from Grandma's rack nearby. The quilts were a relic from an olden time when people hand-crafted blankets with sentimental squares. Each piece was special to Grandma. Her skinny-fingered-fat-knuckled-hands picked over every inch of that blanket.

I pulled the quilt up to my neck as I snuggled into it with foggy exhaustion. Sleep did not immediately come, and I lay in the stillness of the basement blackness thinking about my life. After rolling things around in my head, rest was even further off. The phone conversation with Postitch troubled my thoughts, but there was nothing I could do about it at 3:00 a.m. I figured I'd sleep, then convince Grandpa we needed to leave the next morning.

There is a sleep ritual I learned from Jacob, years prior. He invented it when we were kids, and I used it, without fail, for decades. I imagine I'm an American G.I. in the Arden Forest during the Battle of the Bulge, hiding under three feet of snow. All my fellow soldiers are dead, and the Nazis are advancing through the underbrush. Alone and cold, I find a spot in the forest and build a small, but tidy, log cabin. Carefully, I hide the walls and roof with ferns and branches. Over a few days, with tedious attention, I build a fireplace. I find an old Franklin stove in the woods. There is canned food I pilfered and a few bars of chocolate. Nazi jackboots crunch through the nearby forest thatch. I burrow in my cabin before a roaring fire eating warm food and nibbling a Hershey's bar. It's a strange sleep ritual, but it works every time. In ten minutes, I tumbled into a deep sleep so consuming, my eyes rolled backward into my head.

An hour before dawn, the sound of my name startled me awake. It wasn't my name, not exactly. It was a drawn out, teeth-clenching, whisper in a sotto voce hiss that cut like the nicked blade of a sharp knife. "*Bhaaaab*," the darkness of the basement whispered. Jacob always said "Bha-*aab*" before something god-awful happened. He whispered it to me on the driveway. He whispered it to me with the pigs. He even whispered it to me at Grandma's funeral. He always drew out the syllables, like he was expelling all his breath, the last gasp before he suffocated. He must have died a million little deaths hissing that stupid nickname.

My eyes opened as I laid on the divan staring at the darkness. There was only the VCR light that filled the large basement living room with the faintest tickle of brightness. It was so dark, I couldn't even make out the shapes of the furniture.

An uneasy sensation started then moved to my balls. There was a tickling softness that made me tense up like I was expecting a blow. The hairs on my arms twisted as if electrified. I tried to breathe softly, to listen. That feeling, that gut-wrenching intuition that someone was standing very close hit me like a bucket of freezing water. With my eyes wide and my breath slow, I laid there in the darkness of the basement listening in a trembling paralysis. In that stifling darkness, I wondered if fear could personify itself and touch me with its hands.

The VCR light was like a distant lighthouse on a black ocean. I laid under the covers of Grandma's old quilt looking into the darkness. In an utterly dark room, thoughts and feelings come at you from deep recesses of your own mind. Most times, these thoughts are deflected by inattention and a litany of distractions. In utter darkness, they circle the drain of memory. When no visual stimulus fills the void, the imagination runs wild. I thought about the blood, the grey matter of Jacob's brain splattered in the next room. I thought about how Grandpa avoided all memories of the past, yet he hoarded cheap mementos of trivial events. If there was ever a place where ghosts came to life, where memories of deceased loved ones competed with ten-cent trinkets collected from museums and tourist traps, if the dead returned out of pure spite, it would happen in the basement.

I pulled the quilt up to my nose. My eyes scanned the darkness. More than anything, the words of warning Grandma said on that cold October afternoon repeated in my mind. "Prepare yourself," she warned, "*for what's coming.*"

I laid there on the divan for a half hour full of self-doubt, tottering on the edge of defecation. Perhaps, I thought, the sound was in my head. I wanted to hear it and, of course, I'd psyched myself out. It was all a self-fulfilling prophecy. I came four hundred miles to find it, *and I found it*. Occam's Razor indeed. Amid the darkness, the sound whistled: "Bhaaaaaaaaa."

It came from the corner, directly underneath the TV Jacob loved to watch. The very TV that had implanted so many torturous ideas. I was 100% sure I heard the sound. Those long, drawn-out syllables burned my ears. I sat upright in the darkness with a snap.

I had two choices. I could run up the basement stairs, out the door. But I'd been running my entire life. I yanked the sheet back to put my feet on the shag carpet. I reached out for the coffee table that sat in front of the couch. My fingers extended in the darkness, grasping for purchase. I looked into the corner of the room.

There was a coldness to the basement. Even in the summers, it had a soothing chill. In late October, it was biting cold. When I reached out, the polished wood of the coffee table felt like an ice block. With my fingertips, I pinched the table and pulled myself to the floor. On my hands and knees, I shuffled through the basement like a handicapped canine, wiggle-walking in blackness. The sound, I was sure, came from the far corner. I not only heard it, I felt it seep towards me. The gloom assaulted my senses. For all credit they give to five senses, sight is far and away the lead singer of that quintet. Only when the lead goes down, do you give the other senses unfettered attention. In that blackness, a cacophony of sensations pinged my senses.

I smelled lavender on the air—my grandmother's favorite scent—a chemical odor burned the tip of my tongue. The silence was deafening. Crickets from the garage were gone. The condenser sound had stopped as well. There was, just inches from my face, a deep and consistent flow of air. It was smothered with the thick scent. Like a child who gulps in a massive lungful of breath before going underwater, I swallowed the darkness.

As I neared the corner, there was a pulsing sound, a considerable buildup of tension near my face. I tensed, my jaw clenched, and I squinted my eyes. A palpable fear hung in that room. The memory of Jacob filled the blackness like air in a balloon. My breathing was the first to go. I started pulling frantic gasps. Then my muscles trembled from the tension. I was standing on the precipice of madness, waiting for a gust of wind to blow me into a paranormal chasm.

It hit my face and washed over my nose and mouth like mustard gas. It burned my eyes and lit my taste buds on fire. It blistered the deep recesses of my lungs. The last sense was the sound. That god-awful drawing-out of my name like the tendons of a weak limb pulled beyond its ability. "Bhaaaaaaaaaa . . .."

It was an inch from my face. I felt it inside, and all the years of social awkwardness and pubescent tension came bursting out in a desperate fear-filled scream of terror:

"*Motherfucker!*" I bellowed as I swung into the darkness, connecting with nothing but the smell. My arms flailed as I cleared my lungs. I rose in a crouch with a frog-like jump backward landing in the center of the coffee table. Magazines and books spilled into the alien blackness. Like a baby deer wandering onto an ice-covered lake, I tumbled onto my back, screaming inaudible yips into the dark.

I rose to my feet wreathed in blackness. My lungs were on fire, and I wreaked of lavender so intense I had to squint my eyes. One thought bounced around my head: *get the fuck out*. My first step into the unknown was cat quick. I thought I was in the middle of the room. My next step was instantly wrong. My forehead smashed on the corner of a doorframe. I crumpled to the floor. My hands wrapped around the frame of a door. I knew there was a light switch midway up. My fingers fumbled in the darkness.

After half a second, I found the switch and flipped it on. The room was a disaster. Magazines were strewn about, pages torn from panic. A leg of the coffee table was broken, and shards were spread around the room. I'd knocked over the lamp, and Grandma's handmade quilt rack was in pieces on the floor. Several pictures fell off the wall, and the glass shattered. You had to hand it to me, I thought, I destroyed the room. I made such a ruckus, I expected Grandpa to come pounding down the stairs—like he used to do when Jacob and I were kids—but Grandpa was in a "swamp sleep," far beyond the reach of noise.

My survey of the carnage ended by the corner by the television. The very spot where I felt the presence of Jacob in the darkness. I'd crouched there moments prior, in the blackness, Jacob's deathly breath, I was sure, made the hairs on the back of neck stand up. With the lights on, I saw the source of my fear. Sitting there on the footstool, before the TV, was a white canister that was marked with stickers and flowers. It was about two feet off the ground, which would've been directly pointed at my face when I was crouched.

I grabbed the canister. As I held the painted cylinder away from my face, it sprayed a gentle mist, issuing a delicate sound, "Baaaab," that filled the room with an aroma.

An *automatic air freshener* had caused me to nearly shit my pants and summon the ghosts of my childhood. I almost lost my sanity over the sound of a *fucking* chemical potpourri. A chuckle began in my stomach and rolled to my lungs. *An automatic lavender air freshener*. The chuckle turned into a belly laugh as I set the canister down on the TV stand. I sat on the couch and examined the basement with new confidence. Grandpa was going to be furious about the table and the quilt rack. They were irreplaceable heirlooms he connected with Grandma. I rose then and started stacking books and magazines.

Just as I reached for the shattered table leg. A dull thud came from Grandpa's office.

"Gramps?" I said.

"*GRAMPS?*" I said a little louder. No response.

After the self-inflicted scare I just endured, I wasn't about to work myself up. I walked from the basement living room past the stairs to the office. As I fumbled for the light switch, I had an unsettling feeling. I flipped the light, and I saw Jacob's sweatshirt sitting on the floor. That same shirt that hung on the back of the chair the night he shot himself. For it to be there was an utter impossibility. Yet there it was crumpled on the floor.

I stepped into the office and bent down to examine the sweatshirt. It was the same faded grey hoodie with a silver zipper and blood spots on the chest and parts of the hood. There wasn't a doubt in my mind, it was the same sweatshirt. As I stared, something on Grandpa's desk caught my eye, a subtle twinkle of light.

Hundreds of photographs were tucked under the desk glass: clippings of interesting newspaper articles, pictures of long-dead family members, and mementos from my grandfather's life. I had memorized the tableau of moments—the display had not changed in decades—and I knew exactly where each photo went and the stories behind them. Amid that collection, an unfamiliar paper was tucked underneath the glass cover of the desk.

On closer inspection, it wasn't just any paper. It was my grandfather's stationery. A parchment style paper unevenly colored to give it an antique feel. Through all my graduations: high school, college, and grad school, I'd received a letter written on parchment. Gramps wrote in this cryptic scrawl using a fountain pen. Important letters from him were like reading the Constitution or the Magna Carta. On the desk, I saw a parchment paper, tri-folded, and stuck underneath the glass between a picture of Grandpa bear hugging a political candidate and a newspaper clipping from the Token-Oak Democrat Press about a tragic fire that killed a family of six. On the center of the folded parchment was the unmistakable name "Bha-*aab*."

I reached down to grab the parchment paper, but it was tucked just underneath the glass, and I couldn't pinch a corner. I opened Grandpa's desk drawer and found a paperclip. I shimmied it up against the paper until it came free.

Bha-*aab*,

When someone tries to leave the Hollows, they kill them, and everyone close to them. They are comin' for Gramps, then for you. Believe it or don't. They'll come tonight, and every night until the job is done.

I do not know what they are. But these addicts are spreading throughout the country, through little towns, all controlled from the Hollows. A group of four that runs shit. They've been making dope in the Hollows since the 40s. These four are not people. Not anymore. They can control kids, grade school kids. And during a full moon, stay out of the light, or they will burn you alive. And they know all about you, all about Gramps.

Dogs can sense when they're coming, so they kill off the dogs. Get a dog and trust no one.

The only thing they respect is death. If someone has committed suicide in a building, the addicts will not enter that house, *even at night*. Though they will do anything to draw you out. Don't ever leave a safe house. No matter what. No exceptions. Study the suicides in a town, and you will have a place to hide.

Once the sun goes down, the addicts flip. They murder and burn until dawn. And there are thousands of them in town.

I don't want what happened to me to happen to you and Gramps. It's punishment I wouldn't wish on my worst enemy. Be careful. Be smart. Be strong for Gramps or I will kill you myself.

126

Jacob

After I finished reading, I examined the letter. In my fingertips, the parchment felt electric, like a live wire. A gentle breeze twisted past my face. The parchment paper broke apart in small pieces. A vibrant tornado of glowing squares twisted into the office and vanished into the air like embers from a campfire. I looked on the floor, the sweatshirt was gone. There was nothing but shag carpet and a bunch of knickknacks.

Standing in the middle of the office, I had not taken a breath in half a minute. I inhaled deeply and blinked to re-examine the room. The pieces of parchment paper and the sweatshirt were gone. The rush of adrenaline in my veins slowed. It was almost morning, and I'd barely slept. My arms felt heavy, and my shoulders sagged. Grandpa's office chair was nearby, and I sunk into it with an exhausted flop.

CHAPTER NINE:

DEAD TREES AND BLOWN VEINS

Robert Warrington's Journal
Token-Oak, October 2020
The morning after the Syndemic

From deep in the basement, I heard the unmistakable sound of dogs barking from next door. The Montifusco's bull terrier let out three loud barks. Then another dog, this one more distant, and a third joined in with a chorus of yips. Seconds later, every dog in Lakeside howled. And I remembered Jacob's letter, and the warning listed therein: *they are coming tonight.*

I heard someone screaming, and the sharp boom of a shotgun blast. Three more gunshots then a final exhalation of pain that cut short on the last blast. All sounds tell a story, and that one was the unmistakable wail of death. It wasn't that far off, either. One, maybe two houses down.

A bullpup shotgun sat against the wall of the office near and a box of shells. I grabbed the gun by the barrel and scooped up the ammo. I sprinted up the basement stairs to the kitchen. As I frantically searched the house, the barking outside stopped. A quietness settled over the house as I jogged through. My jaunting stride sounded like a hollow heartbeat.

I walked to Grandpa's room and opened the door. Gramps slept under the covers nestled in the fetal position. Amazing, I thought, how the elderly revert back to children. He looked peaceful, like all the loneliness and uncertainty he carried had drifted away. As I watched him sleep, I knew everything in my life would change

Gramps always slept with his blinds up. He idolized John Wayne and abided by the Duke's "daylight's burning" rhetoric with a religious fervor. When the sun was up, so was Gramps. After Grandma died, Gramps said he had a hard time sleeping. And, consequently, getting up in the morning became a chore. Never in his life had he needed an alarm. "No person," he claimed, "should enter the world to the sound of a machine." He had lived a life straight out of Poor Richard's Almanac, "Early to bed, early to rise, makes a person healthy, wealthy, and wise." He woke up naturally every morning at 6:00 a.m. That all changed after the funeral. Tossing and turning at night, Gramps missed early morning appointments. He refused an alarm, so we'd compromised. Instead, I bought him a clock radio that played CDs. I threw in a Hank Williams album and set the alarm to wake him up every morning to the sound of "*Lovesick Blues.*" The country yodel of Hank Williams singing about heartache filled the bedroom every morning.

I looked out Grandpa's bedroom window at the rooftops of the houses in Lakeside. The full moon hung in the predawn darkness, huge, and larger than I ever remember.

I stood at the window, looking at the yard. The first lights of dawn were beginning to glow in the thunderheads beyond. There was a steady wind, and the branches of the trees overhead thrashed about. Random people started gathering in Grandpa's backyard. Just a few shadowy shapes at first, slipping through a gap in the fence. As I watched, one came immediately after another. In a half minute, there were over two dozen. I started sliding shells into the magazine of the shotgun. The bullpup held fifteen, and I'd loaded it full.

A sound was on the air, and it took me a moment to realize it was the collective breathing from those gathered in the yard. A violent hiss, a seething respiration drifted on the wind. There was a sharpness in their eyes. Many of them were crouched, with fingers spread wide. Several were cut and bleeding. They stood, bent and ready, staring up at the window, waiting.

A new sound, a subtle low whistle cut through the rustling trees like a knife. It was somehow both hollow and piercing at the same time. I had heard it before, some other time in some other place. Heads in the yard bobbed and contorted, searching for the source of the noise. The sound grew louder, and the hollowness of the sound filled the air like a foghorn. The hollow sound became so loud that it felt oppressive, then it completely stopped. I heard a car door close and slam shut

In the back of the yard, the skinhead appeared. He stood, and his horned scalp glistened in the predawn darkness. Nearly fifty people had piled into the yard. The skinhead looked left, then right, and stepped forward. As he walked, he looked up and saw me at the window. It wasn't anger on his face, not quite. Instead, he had a subtle smile, confidence so complete it was awesome to watch.

I steadied the bullpup shotgun and aimed it at the window. The gun was heavy in my hands, with fifteen shells loaded in its magazine. As I brought the gun to my shoulder and stared down the barrel, a nervous twitch spun through my body. The unblinking faces of the people in Grandpa's yard stared back. It was the first time in my life I had ever aimed a gun at a person. Behind their snarling faces, I saw the past and the pain of their struggles. I devoted my life to helping people unpack their problems, to solve the riddle of trauma and addiction. There was sadness in my heart as I scanned the yard with the barrel of the bullpup.

Just then, Grandpa's alarm sparked to life. The face of the clock illuminated in the dark room, and the sound of the CD spinning began. A tinny speaker emitted the sounds of Hank Williams' Lovesick Blues through the room.

I listened to Hank yodel while I palmed the bullpup in my hand. The point of the barrel scanned past the skinhead and stopped. A Cheshire smile spread across his face, so broad it nearly touched his ears. He yelled and motioned forward. The entire yard of people pressed toward the window at the same time in a cryptic, coordinated lurch.

I closed my left eye and hugged my cheek into the barrel of the bullpup. I lined up the sight to the broadest point on the skinhead's chest. My heart was beating so hard I felt I might pass out. The tips of my fingers went numb. A single thought was screaming in my mind, "*If I pull this trigger, I can never go back.*" This would be the end of any normalcy in my life. It would cleave my personality like a blade. I'd seen the effects of trauma on the brain firsthand, and there would be no returning. I pulled in a breath and held it tight as I steadied my arm and widened my feet.

That smile, that huge goddamned smile, glowed back at me. And in those teeth, I saw the reason Jacob had driven home and killed himself. There was a menace behind that enamel that told the whole story. Of the dead dogs and the children of Token-Oak that had succumbed to the people of the Hollows. Decades of families that went missing, thousands of lives destroyed. All in those white incisors were like limestone tombstones. The rotting carcasses along the highways, breadlines, and machine-gun checkpoints across the prairie. I knew it then, what they planned to do with me when they yanked me from the window. They would pull me apart and then move onto Grandpa.

And I squeezed the trigger.

The sound of the gun rang in my ears. Buckshot hit the skinhead's chest, and he tumbled backward. The butt of the bullpup bruised my shoulder, but I didn't stop. I fired two more, catching the skinhead in the shoulder and in the side. His twisting body spun through the remains of the fence and onto the hood of the Lincoln Mark III in the alley.

The crowd stopped and looked backward. The skinhead slid across the hood and disappeared. There was a smear of blood a foot thick in his wake. There was a second of silence and stillness in the yard after the sharp report of the gunshots. I watched the heat drift gently from the tip of the barrel and float out the bedroom window into the cold air. Amid this silence, creeping at the edges, Hank Williams serenaded us from a shrill speaker about beautiful dreams and losing his heart.

The crowd turned, and I opened fire.

The first one to reach the window was only a foot from the barrel. *BOOM.* I hit him in the stomach with a shot so close the wad didn't even spread. I sawed in half as his torso and legs fell backward. *BOOM.* Another, three feet back, caught one in the left knee and his leg exploded. *BOOM.* A third was crouching, and I put another in his left side and one in the palm of his hand, sending fingers spinning into the moonlight. I stopped aiming and unloaded on the crowd. *BOOM. BOOM. BOOM. BOOM.* Firing into the mass of people until the bullpup was empty. The spray of blood and ligaments filled the air like confetti falling at a championship game. Shell casings spun from the chamber.

When the bullpup was empty, there was a U-shaped mass of bodies lying before the window. I had hit twenty-five, maybe thirty addicts. The rest were struggling to climb over the pile. I grabbed the box of shells and started frantically snapping them into the chamber. But they kept coming for the hole in the window. Dozens more rolled past the pile, snarling. In another few seconds, they'd be inside. There were too many, and the calculus became clear. I could shoot a few more with the shells I had loaded, but it would not be enough. They would come through. The inevitability of it all hit me, and I fired once more into the chest of the closest person, sending her heaving backward.

I turned and grabbed Gramps by a shoulder holding the bullpup with the other hand. I yanked him out of his room in such a rush I collapsed on the hallway carpet. He fell as we entered the kitchen. It was then I realized, in my panic, I'd left the rest of the shells in the bedroom on the floor. There were three or four shells in the magazine, but that was it. Maybe I could club a few with the butt of the gun, but there were so many.

I jacked one in the chamber of the shotgun and prepared for the first one to come tearing around the corner of the bedroom. Fuck it, I thought, I'd take a few more in the house and try to get another two. I pulled Grandpa behind me and aimed the bullpup into the darkness of the kitchen. I waited for the first sign of a head, a foot, or fingers curling around a wall... anything to signal they were coming inside.

And I waited.

I could still hear them seething through the back window. The window was wide open, but nobody came. I remember Jacob's letter, something about they can't get inside a house... I peeked around the corner, and I saw dozens standing there. They were thrashing about on top of the corpses, but not one so much as reached inside the window.

I stepped back into the bedroom and looked out. The subtle glow was just above the heads of the addicts in the yard. The sky was still dark, but I saw two pillars of smoke reaching ten thousand feet up. Several fires were burning in town. One was near the center, but the flames were so tall they jumped over the roofs of houses. The grain elevator and the top of the High Rise were on fire. A second blaze burned the next block over. An entire house was lit and smoking furiously. There were random gunshots and sirens all over town.

Near the brick chimney on the neighboring home, two figures were at the peak of the roof. The Montifuscos lived next door in a three-story. The peak of their roof was forty-five feet off the ground, *at least*. One figure stood with arms crossed and another sat crouched nearby. The fires in the distance outlined the silhouettes of their bodies. They might as well be watching a firework display or a shooting star.

The people in the yard stepped backward. They looked up and around and slid away. There was truth to Jacob's statement, I thought, these things cannot come inside. I stepped to the window to get a better look.

When I moved towards the window, I stepped into the fading moonlight cascading through the shattered blinds. The people in the yard were slipping away. Heading back out gaps in the fence and disappearing around corners. Silver light fell across my folded forearms as I watched people disperse. A second after I stepped into the light, the seated figure on the roof stood.

One silhouette raised its arms with its index fingers pointed to the night sky. I felt a tightness in my chest, and a suffocating feeling enveloped my face. The lines of silver on my chest felt uncomfortable, then boiling, and in a few more seconds the skin on my arms seared. The arms of the central figure on the roof shook intensely until my skin smoked. The pungent smell of burning filled the bedroom.

I wanted to pull back out of the moonlight. To shut my eyes from this madness. To wake up in my bed back at home, screaming from fright, only to realize my mind had walked me into this hellish nightmare. It froze me in space so securely, I couldn't even blink. I stared up at the peak of the Montifusco's old Victorian roof. A shape dropped off the roof and disappeared, only to reappear as it pulled down Grandpa's backyard fence.

While shapes were walking away from the house, one headed forward. He was holding a piece of pipe and a lighter in one hand as he disappeared around the side of the house. The shape on the roof lowered its hands, and I fell on to the floor of the bedroom. There were hissing sounds and the twisting of metal. The aroma of rotten eggs filled the air.

I looked up at the roof of the Montifusco's, and the silhouettes disappeared over the back edge of the house. Just before they slid from sight, I had enough time to pull myself behind the foot of Grandpa's bed.

The side of the house exploded into a fireball twenty feet high. The force of the explosion sent patio furniture and hundreds of roof shingles into the air. A black smoke so thick and pure followed the fire. There was a pungent odor. I crawled to the kitchen and found Grandpa huddled in a corner. We sat crumpled on the dirty, sunflower linoleum looking up at the sky through a massive hole in the back of the house.

Grandpa sat upright. He rubbed his neck with his eyes closed. He let out a long breath and looked at me.

"Jacob came home," he said. "He is in the basement again."

"I know, Grandpa," I said.

I jumped up and looked at the neighbor's rooftop again. The shapes on the roof were gone. There were no bodies in the yard. All that remained was freakish wreckage. Fingers and blood sat on top of the snow. The early morning wind gusted through the massive hole in the back of the house, blowing my hair back. They may not come in, I thought, but that wouldn't stop them from destroying the place.

"What the hell happened?" Gramps said, looking out the aperture.

We both sat on the kitchen floor, looking out at the carnage in the yard. Bushes and trees around the house were still on fire. Specks of ash fell from the sky, mixed with thousands of burning dead leaves. I hadn't noticed before, but all the oaks above Grandpa's house were lifeless. Their bare limbs pointing in a hundred directions.

Gramps scowled as he watched the fire. Then he slumped into a chair on the kitchen table. I approached him, but he waved me off. *"Check to see,"* he said, holding his stomach and coughing, "check to see if more are coming. Check the town." I bounded up the stairs to the second floor. There was a bedroom window that led out onto the roof. I shimmied the warped wood of the old window and slid through a crack just big enough to fit my head. The front of my pants tore as I wiggled onto the old shake shingle rooftop.

I climbed the peak of the roof and took in a breath. The sun was rising on the eastern horizon. Towers of black smoke were all around, and an eerie haze filled the air. I was looking west across Heart Swallow Lake. The county jail was smoldering from a fire. There was a hole in a northern wall of the jail, and two police cruisers were burning on Main Street. Small fires were everywhere. There were other people on rooftops all across Lakeside. Several had hunting rifles with scopes and were sweeping through the smoke looking for someone to shoot. Dozens of people were on the roof of the High Rise looking down in a panic as smoke rolled out the windows of a lower floor. Every few seconds, there was a sharp report of a rifle.

A body was strewn across the middle of the intersection of Main Street and MLK. One of its arms was shorn clean and laying on the sidewalk. A mess of innards was strung in front of the body in a ghastly pattern. There were two dead kids on the railroad tracks. And in front of the Fair Grounds, a pile of people laid covered in blood—four or five, but it could have been more. They were blended into each other like a demented game of Twister. There were pickup trucks strung along the length of MLK, smashed into poles and flipped over. The drivers of the vehicles were dead inside or nearby walking in a shocked daze.

It was madness everywhere. As I pivoted on the peak of the roof, I saw two wrecked fire trucks in front of the Token-Oak Zoo. There was a police cruiser upside down and on fire. At first glance, it seemed like absolute pandemonium. Then something that made my heart skip a beat.

The telephone wires that ran along the railroad tracks were laying on the street. The telephone poles at the end of every street in town were cut down. The principal road that connected Token-Oak to the interstate had two semi-trucks overturned, and a dozen cars smashed into a colossal pile. The entrance into Token-Oak from the east was similarly restricted. There was a three-hundred-foot cell tower to the northeast, in the field behind Jacob's shop, laying on its side, reduced to twisted metal wreckage.

Underneath the chaos, there was a system. There was no one to call and nowhere to go. In this little city, at least for the next day, no one would be coming to help. It was crazy, so surreal that I expected to wake up in a cold sweat. I pulled my phone out my pocket and confirmed I had no signal. I looked into the windows of the houses around Lakeside and did not see a single light.

Fat flakes of fresh snow started poking through the smoke. A reminder of other problems on the horizon. There would be no electricity tonight. It was going to be cold and dark. The house, with such a hole in the back wall, would be freezing. The water pump wasn't going to work. If this went longer than a day, food would be an issue, too. A little panic settled over me then, thinking about all the things I had to do.

I looked at the backside of the house from the roof. From above, there were parts of people spread out on the snow. I blinked hard and looked again. I'd emptied the bullpup, and I was sure I'd dropped at least fifteen. Maybe not killed that many, but severely winged several. The bodies were *gone*. The semi-circle of blood and blown off flesh contrasted so sharply with the white snow.

Near the back fence, the Lincoln Mark III was gone, too. I looked under the dead trees and all around the edges of the house. I put two shots in that skinhead's chest and another in the side of his ribs. But he had disappeared. I stopped for a moment and breathed silently as I looked at the spot where he fell.

The Skinhead would be back that night, I could feel it. As it was late October, sunset would be around 6:30. As I figured it, I had less than ten hours to collect supplies. I had to scrounge up some ammunition, water, food, and then decide how Grandpa and I would leave Token-Oak. We couldn't stay in the house even if Jacob was right and they wouldn't go inside. We had to run. Though how far could I get with an elderly man in tow.

I looked up at the Hollows. The hillside was filled with smoke. The forest of dead trees was utterly dark. Upon the hilltop, however, there was a massive blaze burning. The wind whipped and snapped the tall flames in many directions as the fire burned above Token-Oak like the very pits of hell.

At first, it was a distant hunch, an uncomfortable thought. Then it became a guarantee. Whatever those things were last night, they came from the Hollows. I'd known it for a long time, maybe all the way back to when I was a kid. All the way back to Grandma's driveway. Somewhere in those meth-addled eyes of that addict.

In the distance, a police siren bleated. A car pulled around the pile of vehicles at the east end of MLK. The old Bronco had huge tires and the lights of his siren sent pillars of flashing light through the smoke. The Bronco swerved around overturned cars along the road. The car took a left on Main Street, and a distinctly female officer yelled into the bullhorn. "People of Token-Oak, stay in your homes! Lock your doors!" The Bronco pulled onto the lawn of the courthouse and disappeared behind the clocktower from my view.

People scampered off their roofs into windows. One of the houses nearby opened their front door, and three people walked across the lawn, the tips of their rifles shined in the early morning sun. A group of ten, similarly armed, walked out of the back of Zion Lutheran Church and moved towards the center of town. Dozens more left their homes and headed for the courthouse. All were carrying guns.

I ran through the house yelling to Grandpa, "I am headed to the center of town! Everyone is. Stay here. I'll be back." He wasn't in the kitchen anymore and didn't immediately answer. "Gramps!" I yelled louder. "STAY HERE!" I waited for him to answer, but nothing came. I couldn't wait, so I ran down the kitchen stairs and out the back door with the bullpup ready to fire.

Once I hit the street, Bill Montifusco was dead on his front lawn. His bathrobe was open, and someone had cut him open from his stomach to his neck. A shiver of fear hit me. I moved against the houses underneath the trees, walking through gardens and flower beds, doing my best to stay hidden.

I was standing underneath a tree, hiding behind a garden trellis, watching people cross the street towards Zion Lutheran. If they made it without getting shot, I thought, I'd go, too. Then I felt the hard circle of a shotgun press into my back.

"I just wohrtered my azaleas, fuckstick. Breathe, and I'll spread your guts like a can of pizza sauce." The voice, absolutely alien to the slow Midwest drawl of Token-Oak, was pure east coast. "Put da piece on the ground, get on ya knees, and tell me who won the series last year."

"What?" I said.

"The series, bitch. Who won it last year?" the voice said.

"I don't watch baseball!"

The man walked around from behind me. It was Jonnie Terabaso, my old childhood friend. I hadn't seen him since I was ten years old, back when we used to play basketball on the court near the High Rise. Jonnie was a Midwest transplant and, apparently, never lost his Jersey accent or attitude. He pulled me up off my knees and gave me a hug.

"Damn, Jonnie, I thought you were going to shoot me for sure."

"*I was*," he said with a wry smile. "Spread open four or five last night right here. I saw a shadow in the window, figured they were back." He looked up, and several people were walking across the street, carrying guns. "What the fuck? Where is everyone goin'?"

I told him what about the cop car. "There are people headed in that direction from nearly every street."

"I'm goin' too," Jonnie said. He rubbed the back of his head with his hand. He looked concerned as his eyes scanned up and down the street.

"What?" I said.

"My daughtah, she can't stay here. We've got no powah and the wohrter went out last night. She's a tough kid, but I ain't askin' her to stay alone. Not aftah last night."

Jonnie walked over to the side of his house and whistled. A little girl emerged from the door. Her hair was up in a ponytail, and she wore shoes that lit up on the heel with every step she took. She stood right behind her dad. She'd inherited Jonnie's perpetually earnest expression. As kids, we used to joke he always looked pissed, like he was about to tell somebody to eat shit. She had on a backpack and was holding a child-sized shotgun with both hands.

"Gigi, this is Robby. We grew up together. Stay close, sweetheart. Right behind me. We're goin' ovah the courthouse for a few minutes. Then we are comin' right back. Understand."

Gigi nodded, and her eyes started looking around the neighborhood.

The girl shook my hand, and we started walking. We crossed the street by Zion Lutheran. There were fires everywhere. There was a car flipped over at the east end of the road and two mangled bodies lay on the asphalt. Just past the church, the top floors of the High Rise were disgorging smoke. Several alarm systems were going off in a discordant screech. A woman was sobbing over the lifeless body of a loved one in the open field of the church.

"Jesus," Jonnie said, "stay close, sweetheart."

As we moved across Main, the wind caught the smoke and blew it in our faces. It was a chemical smell, like burning rubber and fuel. In the distance, the grain elevators were still burning hot.

We kept moving across the street until we reached the courthouse. As we angled around the side of the building, we saw a group of several hundred people standing under the Token-Oak. The police officer had parked the Bronco under the tree and was standing on the running board of the truck talking to the crowd with a megaphone.

"That is Betty Ripsome," Jonnie said. And we moved through the crowd until we were under the tree. Officer Ripsome had her palms up and fingers spread, before I even heard her speak, I could tell she was trying to calm the crowd.

"Now, listen," Officer Ripsome said in a commanding tone. "I don't know what happened last night…"

"Then what the fuck are we doing down here," a voice from the crowd yelled.

"Right now, the best thing to do is to go to your homes and sit tight. Lock the doors and load your weapons. I'm going to make some calls. We will get a response team here ASAP. Chief Miller…"

"Chief Miller is laying on Main with his guts pulled out," an angry man with coveralls and a Stetson hat said, stepping forward. "Officers Brady and another are burnt to death in a patrol car over on Halstead. McMillian got her throat pulled apart. What the hell is going on?"

"I don't know," Officer Ripsome said, holding back tears, "I was over in Chickamauga Basin when I got the calls. I got here as fast as I could. Right now, if everyone would just go home and …"

"I was in my home, and one of those goddamn things busted in and killed my wife," a young man wearing a mechanic's uniform said. "They even killed my dog."

"God, Russ, *I'm sorry*," Officer Ripsome said, holding her mouth.

Shocked faces stood still all around me. There were people under the Token-Oak and standing on the benches in the square. The courthouse steps were full. Families, much like Jonnie, had traveled together to listen to the news. Everyone, even the little kids, had a rifle or a shotgun. The smoke in the air wafted about in thick strands, forcing most of the people to cover their mouths with a cloth. The fear in the air was palpable, so intense that it made me shiver.

All these people collected underneath the massive branches of the Token-Oak. Its bare limbs, curled over the heads of the crowd, providing an eerie ceiling of dead wood. The old oak had not lost its symmetrical beauty, and its lower branches covered the group of two hundred like the bony fingers of a parent reaching into a crib to swaddle a baby. I watched the smoke and ash wash the outstretched fingers of that oak in an apocalyptic shower.

The man with the Stetson hat stepped forward and looked out at the crowd. He pulled himself up onto the Bronco so he could stand next to Betty Ripsome. He looked out onto a sea of confused faces, the smoke from the fires making everyone squint. "No offense, Betty," he said, "but I'm not going back home. I ain't felt the least bit safe until I got here under this tree." He paused a minute and looked around.

"I don't know what those things are. But I know where they are. I watched hundreds of them running past McClintock's this morning up to the Hollows."

A chorus of agreement sprung up from the crowd. Validated, the man pressed forward. "There are enough of us here, enough guns in our hands, that we could go up there and put an end to this today. This town has dealt with those speed freaks long enough."

A boy near the back of the crowd caught my attention. His head tilted slightly to the left, and his face lost all expression. He swiveled backward and walked away from the ruckus. His father was yelling and did not notice. The boy walked in a weird rhythm, without moving his arms. I stood on my tiptoes but could not find the boy over the crowd. While I stood under the Token-Oak, looking for the boy, I remembered the kids on the court years prior. I thought back to the day of Jacob and the pigs. A breath caught in my chest, and I gulped hard.

"Now, just wait a minute," Officer Ripsome said to the man in the Stetson, "what are you going to do up there, RC? This is not the frontier; that's illegal. If you go up there, you're going to get killed or end up inside this courthouse in shackles waiting for trial."

"You tell that to the parents of the boy lying on Main with his throat ripped out. Or to the family of those cops still burning on Halstead." The crowd under the old oak roared in agreement. A few fists went up into the air.

"Ain't nobody going to convict me in this town," RC said with his chest puffed out. "No way in hell."

"You won't be tried here, RC. None of you will," Officer Ripsome said. *"Go home! Lock your doors! Help will come!* Those that did this will be *arrested, charged,* and *convicted.* Trust the process."

"Fuck the process!" RC screamed to the crowd. The crowd exploded with agreement. And any hesitation the crowd had was lost when RC racked his shotgun and fired it once into the air. "I'm going up there, and I ask y'all to come with me. Any dope fiend I see will be put down. Fuck a trial, I ain't going to sit around waiting for the 'process' to run its course. I say we deal with that shit right now."

I felt it in my stomach first, a subtle sensation of movement. I looked above my head, and the branches of the Token-Oak were swaying gently. Not only the tips in the wind, but the thick lower limbs were undulating like the slithering belly of a snake crawling across the floor. There was the sound of dead wood squealing, barely audible under the noise of the crowd. As I looked a foot above my head, the weight of the old tree seemed to crush down on the crowd.

"We need to go," I said to Jonnie. *"Right now."*

RC raised his shotgun in the air and shook it over the crowd. They were worked into a thick lather, ready to follow him into the depths of the Hollows. RC's neck was taught cables and veins as he growled into the throng. He jumped down from the running board of the Bronco ready to lead.

The minute he hit the ground, the top of RC's head exploded into a fine mist. An amazed expression slid across RC's face like a pencil rolling off a table. He slumped to the grass underneath the Token-Oak. His body hit the fescue with a dull thud.

I looked and saw Gigi holding her 410 staring down at RC's body. The smell of burnt powder wafted from the barrel of her gun. Gigi dropped her weapon and looked up at me with empty eyes.

Another shot rang out, and Officer Ripsome grabbed her chest and slid off the Bronco. A third shot and one of the most vocal people in the crowd moaned and fell to the grass. A young boy stood before both bodies holding a double-barreled Winchester.

There was a long pause, and everyone in the vicinity looked on. It was a confused moment, a series of events so unexpected that the entire courthouse square stood in utter shock.

Jonnie grabbed Gigi and turned. The lights of her heels flashing as her little legs flailed in the air. She was screaming like a child who had woken from a horrible nightmare.

We pressed backward through the crowd and ran. There was another loud pop and another. In a moment, it seemed a volley of booms filled the square. I didn't look backward. Instead I followed Jonnie as he broke for the corner of the courthouse.

As we reached courthouse running towards Main, there was a massive explosion. We stopped for a moment and looked back. A fireball reached hundreds of feet into the air and folded into itself in a mushroom shape that rose above the courthouse lawn like a spectral demon ascending into the morning air.

The fireball was so large it enveloped the Token-Oak. The dead branches igniting in lines of flames. The old tree's limbs writhed in a desperate wriggle like the flaming human limbs.

"My God!" Jonnie said, "Oh my God!"

And we ran back to Lakeside with Token-Oak popping and burning all around us.

We made it back to Grandpa's house in less than a minute. Jonnie carried Gigi over his shoulder, sprinting the entire way with one hand on her back and the other holding two shotguns. We hit the back door of Grandpa's house and slammed it shut behind us.

I saw immediately that the kitchen stairs were covered in blood. There were large chunks of flesh on the top of the stairs and a trail of smeared blood leading out the back door. My knees buckled, and I grabbed the kitchen counter to keep from falling.

"Grandpa! GRANDPA! *GRANDPA!*" I yelled. I ran through the house throwing open doors to empty rooms.

"We cannot stay here," Jonnie said, meeting me in the living room hallway.

"I have to find him," I said. "I cannot leave an elderly man wandering around Token-Oak."

"Robbie, he's dead. All that blood... I'm sorry. Lots of good people died last night."

Jonnie ran up and hugged me.

"Gigi and I are not staying in this town. Those things are coming back. You're not Mr. Current Events, but I've seen the roads heading out of town.

They are riddled with bodies. It's a nightmare. And whatever is going on, it's in people, maybe all people. We need to *get the hell out of here*. Out into the prairie, into the woods."

Jonnie explained that he had a bugout kit at his house, a stash of rifles, and a ton of freeze-dried food. He said with a tingle of embarrassment that he wasn't a prepper, he was only prepared for something to happen. About thirty miles out of town, on the upper escarpment in Chickamauga Basin, he had a hunting cabin full of supplies. He had 500 gallons of propane and a water well.

"If we can make it to my cabin, we can make it for weeks. If we are careful, maybe even months. Nobody knows about it. It's on six-hundred acres that a distant uncle owns. It's secluded. It's safe. But we *must leave here now*," Jonnie said. "We get out there and wait for the government to sort this out. But we *have to leave now*."

There was a string of gunshots outside. There was a sharp scream. It all sounded a few blocks away. There was a palpable sensation that no place in town would be safe, guns or not.

"We get out there and wait for the government to sort this out. But we *have—to—leave—now*," Jonnie said again with wide eyes while staring into my face.

I wanted to tell Jonnie about the addicts, the experiment, about meeting Postitch at Scotts Bluff, Nebraska, in three weeks. Most of all, I wanted to tell him about the kids. Gigi had shot a person in the center of town. One of them, the big man with the cowboy hat, was surely dead. Now was not the time.

"If the roads are blocked..." I said looking out a window, "and we have to stay away from people, what do you suggest? Even if we get out of here, there are more towns, every farmstead will have more people."

Jonnie expected this question and answered it quickly, "We walk it. It's the only way to stay hidden."

"*Walk*! In this shit? You can't be serious."

"Look, we use the main storm sewer. It's forty-eight inches wide and runs through the center of town. It drops into the banks of the Smokey. There is a manhole in some pampas grass in my backyard that connects to the line. We drop in and hit the river. Then we walk the banks of the Smokey, staying in the trees, walking under cover of cottonwoods. No one will see us. People will assume we are dead."

I looked at Jonnie, and he was looking down at Gigi. He bent down and hugged her close, and she hugged him back. I realized that Jonnie wanted to leave Token-Oak for his little girl. Sure, he was freaked out, and he was right, going was the right thing to do. What he didn't say, and I saw as he hugged her, was that he wanted to get Gigi out of town to sort things out. He didn't intend to come back.

Gigi held him close and looked up at me while she held her dad. The hair tie on her ponytail was coming lose. She had a smear of dirt on her face. Every time there was a gunshot outside, her little head would duck. The hair on her ponytail shook with each shiver. I reached down and put my hand on her head.

"Alright," I said, "let's go. But if we do this, we do it quickly."

In less than five minutes, we were standing on the back porch of Jonnie's house. Each of us was carrying a backpack and a shotgun. We walked across the yard to the storm sewer entrance. It was like Jonnie said, a concrete embankment surrounded by pampas grass. Jonnie jumped up, and I handed him Gigi. I jumped up and stood near the manhole cover.

Jonnie grabbed a tool and pulled the manhole cover free. The sliding metal made a hollow gulping sound as it slid open. As I looked down into the blackness, it looked like a mouth about to swallow us whole.

In the moments before we slid down into the darkness of the storm sewer, I looked around Token-Oak. I could only see the tops of things over neighborhood fences. The tallest structures in town—the High Rise, the steeple to Zion Lutheran Church, the grain elevators, and the top of the Ferris wheel—were all burning. Gunshots popped every few moments in all directions. The rotten egg smell of gas filled the air. A purple smoke made everything seem vague and ephemeral. Token-Oak was a living hell. There was a pressure above like God himself had snapped a lid on top of the town to increase the heat of the burn.

As I handed Gigi into the storm sewer to her father, she was crying.

"It will be OK," I whispered to her as I handed her off below.

"Will it?" she said while looking into my face with a straightforwardness that caught me short.

I nodded and gave her a half-hearted smile.

When I wiggled my way down, the cool air of the underground tickled my skin. Once I pulled the manhole cover shut over our heads, we stood in the darkness of the pipe. The world above was a hushed memory, it felt far off. The three of us turned to walk toward the Smokey River. Our shoe soles splashed in the standing water at the bottom of the pipe. The halogen lantern in Jonnie's hands cast our shadow onto the concave of the wall behind us like a trio of misshapen ghosts that were doomed to haunt the underground.

We splashed our way towards the Smokey in the darkness of the storm sewers under Token-Oak. The cement tube was full of piles of damp leaves. Little mountains of moist death that we had to navigate around. Leaves from the hundreds of bare trees, their dead branches above us, and their dead roots wrapped around the pipe that we walked. The roots of those dead trees had broken through the cement and hung like dead snakes in our path. All the while, I could smell ammonia and hear the crunch of hypodermic needle casings crushing under our feet as we walked in the darkness towards the Smokey.

KILL HOLLOWS

AUTHOR NOTES

S.D. Lifter is, of course, a pseudonym. The genesis of the name came—and this will sound a little strange for an author of dark thrillers—from gardening. One of my favorite tomato breeds is the *Mortgage Lifter*. The story behind this tomato begins in the Great Depression. Apparently, a gardener in Appalachia crossbred tomatoes to make the *Mortgage Lifter*. The gardener—let's call him the "Lifter"—prolifically sold his new breed and successfully paid off his mortgage during a bleak economic time. The Lifter pursued his passion and "lifted" his burden. What a great story and a damn tasty tomato.

I, too, understand the burden of a debt. My wife and I have over two hundred thousand in student loans. A collective debt so large and oppressive that, even with regular large payments, we will never pay them off. Therefore, my pseudonym, is **S**tudent **D**ebt **L**ifter. And my dream is to lift the burden of this debt through writing. I fully acknowledge it's a terrible plan, but it's my plan and I will give it my best shot.

As for my story, I grew up in central Kansas. My family had a 500-acre farm outside of town that raised wheat and dabbled in livestock. At a young age, my parents moved our family to Kansas City. We left the small confines of rural Kansas, though, I returned every summer for a few weeks well into adulthood. Every time I went back, a little piece of the town had died. Business disappeared. Prosperous parts of the local economy faded. There was always an increasing bitterness among the townsfolk about the decline. Though most of them were too deeply connected to a local business or the land to leave.

There are memories of my hometown that I carry with me. The way people raise just a finger when driving past on country roads. How courthouse square was teaming with small-town business in my youth. Little things such as the popping of fireworks in the middle of the street in July and the taste of the Blizzards at the local Dairy Queen. The smell of golden stalks of wheat as they spun into a combine header during harvest. I remember the grain elevators and the feed lots and the crops dusters buzz bombing fields like Kamikaze pilots just barely missing telephone wires. Every time I walk into tallgrass, I still feel the pinching fingers of two-inch grasshoppers on my neck.

Most of all, though, I remember the drugs. As a kid, in the 1980s, drugs were in the background, a guilty thought passed between friends. Back then, small town drugs were just a bit of rust on the running boards of an otherwise nice pickup. By the 1990s the decaying fingers of that rust had reached a little further. By the time I had grown into a man, around 2000, it wasn't wheat or oil or cattle that was the chief export of my hometown; it was meth. And the stuff was everywhere. There was not a single family in town that was not affected by the epidemic at some level. Like so many, I moved away just as the surge of methamphetamines took over. The 100-person capacity county jail filled up with inmates and, it seems, it has been overflowing since the first Bush was in office.

When I got out of law school, I returned to Kansas and work with an energy company as a landman/in-house attorney. T. S. Eliot said, and I may get this wrong, that we should never cease from exploring, and at the end of our travels, we will arrive at the place where we first started and see the place for the first time. I saw rural America in a new light. My job took me to desolate places throughout the state. Windswept towns so isolated that they didn't have a single fast food establishment. I traveled the backeddys of Kansas and came to understand the secret rhythms of the state. There were trips to the Arrikaree Breaks, Castle Rock, and Monument Rock. I spent time in caverns and walking the red hills. I floated rivers such as the Smokey and the Saline. I fell in love with the Great Plains all over again.

Two years out of law school, I went into private practice and my geographical reach spread into Nebraska, eastern Colorado, the panhandle of Oklahoma, and into other remote places. As an adult, I saw these places through new lenses of experience and education. For a brief period, I took criminal appointments in district courts where there were not enough local attorneys to defend the accused. Along the way, the seeds of the Token-Oak series grew.

Token-Oak is an every town, a collection of rural towns in I've visited in the Midwest. These little towns, unequivocally, revolve around a county courthouse a with a police station within a block. These are places where local sports are as big a backbone of the local culture as the Lutheran church. There is always a Dairy Queen or a Tasty Freeze. There are neighborhoods socioeconomically segregated that include trailer parks, old cinderblock houses, older well-built homes, and a smattering of mansion-style builds for the local aristocrats. Grain elevators, a feed lot, and a local slaughterhouse are ever-present. The local nightlife comprises the animals of small-town hootch hounds—the Elks, Moose, the Eagles—and there is always one seedy watering hole with cheap liquor and illicit drugs. Main Street in every single one of these places is a living history that shows the power of the past and uncertainty of the future on the Great Plains.

There is a beauty to these towns that I've tried to convey in *Kill Hollows*. The same beauty that comes marveling at a wooden schooner intricately built inside a bottle. In places so remote, there is often the incredible sensation just miles outside of town of the unexplored, the undiscovered. There is a fortitude among the people in these rural vistas, a resilience that is infective. These places are unquestionably challenging to live in, but in these towns, there are genuine artists beyond the influence of city culture and mainstream personalities. Many of these characters have infused the pages of this book.

Underneath all of this, in too many of these places, is methamphetamines. Users roam country roads at night at top speed looking for something to steal. They cook drugs using a dangerous cocktail of locally available chemicals. The police stations in these small towns are overflowing with addicts. At district courthouses on "motion days" one can still see the chain gang of orange jumpsuit addicts shuffling into court for a hearing. There are lab explosions and most small-town hospitals have a handful of chemical burn stories that seem more appropriate in a WWI trench.

Recently, the opiate crisis hit these towns, too. The data on this second epidemic is terrifying. The true effects of the crisis have come in the form of suicides and extreme medical bills. Big Pharma is feasting on the poorest towns in America and this is just the beginning. The future in these places is bleak now and getting progressively worse every single year. In the coming years, there will indeed be an apocalyptic future for rural America, a hellish forecast that is just now coming into view.

More than anything, it was apparent the system had failed rural America. Meth precursors could be legally banned. Pharmaceutical opiates could be chemically altered to remove the insane high. Drug programs in court are geared less towards true rehabilitation and more towards are perpetual revenue generation. Make no mistake, the government failed small town America and continues to do so at every turn. *Kill Hollows* began with a simple premise: what if the government tried to control addiction through inhumane field testing on the American people. This is, of course, a work of fiction, though the truth of this drug epidemic apocalypse is not far from the truth.

I am left to wonder what will become of middle America in the next fifty years. The jobs have already gone. People cling to the edges in these remote places. Vital industries, such as medicine, agriculture, and the law are disappearing. However, most of the people in these areas were grandfathered in. They come from generations of small-town doctors, small firms, or the family farm. It's rare for new industries to spring up, and rarer still for a vibrant economy to exist on the Great Plains. There are desperate times already, and the future looks even worse. Someone far smarter than I will have the answers to this conundrum. There is a solution to this problem, if only we have the courage to see it.

This is my first novel. I hope to publish a new book in this series every three months. It's a lofty goal for a young attorney working sixty hours a week, with two small children, a wife, and to big dogs that need exercise. Nonetheless, I plan to stick to that goal over the next four years. So please check back on my Amazon page every few months.

If you get a chance, please review this work. Beyond the impossible goal of paying off my student debt, I really love writing stories that people enjoy. There is not greater satisfaction for me than just a simple note from a reader of my fiction that enjoyed the story. Stories, after all, are what we live for, what we die for, they are who we are. I love telling them more than anything. So please, if you are so inclined, drop me a review when you have the time. If you are bolder, do not hesitate to reach me by email at contact@sdlifter.com. I will get back to you when time permits.

KILL HOLLOWS

CREDITS AND THANKS

There are numerous people that helped bring this book to fruition, each of them spread out across the United States.

First, to my wife Abby who has been soapboxing for this book to be done for years. Frankly, I have talked about it so much that my wife finally reverted to saying just "publish the damn thing already." Abby was incredibly supportive of my writing habit along the way. She brought me a desktop and helped me set up a place in the house where I could write. More than anything, she spent years listening to my handwringing and insecurities of getting book to the finish line. Thank you, sweetheart. You are an amazing woman and I am lucky to have you.

Second, to my two kids, Lily and Lincoln. One of the biggest reasons that I wrote this book is I want you to follow your dreams. Who am I to tell you to "let it rip" when I didn't have the courage to do it myself? No matter what you do in life, there will always be someone there to tear you down. I didn't write this book—or any book, for that matter—for years because I was afraid. I feared failure and what people would think. Writing fiction, after all, is an exceptionally personally endeavor. I am now embarrassed that it took me so long to get it out. The joy I have from the effort that I put into

151

the book, far outweighs any fear I had going in. In the future, you will both be faced with a similar situation. Do not be afraid to fail, or you will never give yourself the chance to succeed.

Then there is my friend, and lifelong fan of dark thrillers, J.B. Rigga. JB has a home in the Arikaree Breaks of Kansas. A carpenter by trade with a business moto that reads "I'm slow and expensive," JB spends his days patrolling the backroads of rural America near the border Colorado, Kansas, and Nebraska. A true renaissance man with a passion for nature and healthy living. JB is a collector of great memories in the backwoods. I came to know him when I worked as a landman scouting well locations. One of the first times we ever hung out, JB drove me to a remote spot on private land near in the Arikaree Breaks. We walked from his pickup into a natural cavern that stretched a hundred feet wide and fifty feet tall. It was a place, no doubt, that the Plains Indians viewed as a holy shrine. When we entered the mouth of the cavern, JB solemnly called for a minute of silence. I stood there with a Coors yellowbelly in my hand and listened. Now, JB didn't ask me to listen, but I heard the history of that place, and that hidden cavern ignited a fire in me to write a book that has never been extinguished. JB, thank you for the hours of editing. The endless corrections and nights on the phone. Most of all, thank you for showing me the hidden beauty of rural America.

To my dear friend Joe Cherveny from Austin, Texas. Joe has read everything and has an eye for bullshit. His mind is as sharp as a serial killer scouting victims to kill. I came to know Joe when we worked at a sleep lab together in Austin while I was attending the university of Texas. Joe managed the lab and let me run wild during the nights. Our lab was a veritable pirate ship of madness, complete with the most colorful cast of characters that I have ever known. Joe is former jazz pianist that once ran an internet collective of wolf enthusiasts that filled chat rooms keyboard howls (*"ARH-WOOOOOOOOOOOOOOOOOOOOOO"*). He is a true badass in every respect and spent hours editing this work. Thank you, Joseph, you are a gem of a man.

To my law school friend, Spencer. A Utah native that attended BYU for undergrad, Spencer is brilliant. Spence once had a contracts professor tell him he wrote the best final exam he'd ever read. Spencer has a huge heart and is one of those rare people that just gets it. Thanks for reading my book and giving me pointers. Spence told me, what parts worked and what parts didn't.

To Jesse Williams out of Tulsa. An engineer by trade with a mind like a steel trap, Jesse brought a wholly unique set of eyes to Token-Oak and I will be forever grateful for the tips. He is a bastion of great ideas and a good friend.

Penultimately, to Jerome Bump, the finest professor that I have ever encountered. I was blessed to take Victorian Literature and Animal Humanities with Professor Bump while at the University of Texas. According to Professor Bump, writing with emotion should not be discouraged, but utilized. "Hammer your thoughts into unity." I still remember setting around the fire at Professor Bump's home in the Texas Hill Country and discussing life. While a student in Professor Bump's class, I wrote a shorty story about my father's passing as told through the eyes of one of my pets. A former student told me that Professor Bump used that story for several years as an example of good emotional writing to incoming freshman. Thank you, professor, you are a living legend.

Finally, to my father Richard Titus. My father loved to read history books and, just before he passed, he said that his greatest regret was not pursing his dream of becoming a history teacher. He told me to chase my dreams, the ones that really mean something. My dream was this book, and the books that are sure to follow.

Made in the USA
Las Vegas, NV
12 June 2021

24649127R00100